THE BRIDGEMAN

AN EMILY TAYLOR MYSTERY

CATHERINE ASTOLFO

THE BRIDGEMAN

An Emily Taylor Mystery - Book 1

Copyright © 2012 by Catherine Astolfo. All Rights Reserved.

No part of this publication may be reproduced, stored in a retrieval system, or transmitted, in any form or by any means, electronic, mechanical, photocopying, recording, or otherwise, without prior written permission from the authors.

This is a work of fiction. Names, characters, places and incidents either are the product of the author's imagination or are used fictitiously. And any resemblance to actual persons, living, dead (or in any other form), business establishments, events, or locales is entirely coincidental.

http://www.catherineastolfo.com

SECOND EDITION trade paperback

Imajin Books - http://www.imajinbooks.com

April 10, 2012

ISBN: 978-1-926997-62-9

Cover designed by Sapphire Designs - http://designs.sapphiredreams.org

Praise for The Bridgeman

"Love and depravity, rebirth and rot, veneer and the real wood underneath—Astolfo brings these opposing forces into play as she creates the complex community that is Burchill. Ordinary people find themselves in an extraordinary situation. Astolfo reveals their personalities in delicious detail." —Garry Ryan, author of the *Detective Lane Mysteries*

"Master storyteller Cathy Astolfo pulls out all the stops as old secrets come back to kill…in this chilling story of twisted desires. Astolfo grabs small-town Ontario and shakes it until its ugly secrets pour out. You won't catch your breath until the last page turns." —Lou Allin, author of *She Felt No Pain*

"Catherine Astolfo's descriptive prose and well-crafted characters soon make you feel part of the community of Burchill, sharing Emily's terror at what is happening in her perfect little town. It's a story rich in detail with unexpected twists and turns that keep you involved right through to the shocking end." —Meredith Henderson, actress, film producer, poet

"Astolfo throws opens the door of her idyllic setting into a world of darkness, depravity, and danger...After reading The Bridgeman, you'll want to go home, lock the doors, and hug your pet." —Anthony Bidulka, author of the Russell Quant Mystery Series

This book is dedicated to my family, friends and colleagues, who bought me the desk and encouraged me to realize my dream.

Acknowledgements

My husband Vince, my best friend, my heart, and my soul mate. Without him, I could never have accomplished any of this. Vince also did a lot of the research on policing in Ontario—any errors are completely mine.

Kristen is not only my beloved daughter, but she is my friend and my inspiration. Writing has always been my dream and she has been the key in realizing it. She has such a talent for promoting others—I hope she appreciates how special and amazing she is, too.

James, my adored son, is a gifted, intelligent source of delight and pride. He will continue to make a difference in the world. His wife, Meredith, is my second daughter, ma belle-fille, my heart.

Without my mother Maureen's encouragement, support, and love, I'd be lost. My sisters and families, who love me and whom I love so fiercely in return, I will always be grateful for your influence in my life.

My stepsons and families have given me such happiness with their acceptance and affection.

My beautiful grandchildren are such a source of joy and wonder; they keep me balanced and in awe of this wonderful life.

My best friends have been my first editors, readers and supporters—they are family, too.

Thanks to Brian Pemberton, of the Ontario Society of the Prevention of Cruelty to Animals, and my niece Meghan Straw for information regarding puppy mills. Any errors are strictly mine.

Thank you to Cheryl Tardif and Imajin Books for believing in Emily and me, and for her indefatigable support of Canadian writers.

PROLOGUE

Discovering a dead body in the basement of a small school in the midst of a quiet village is not something anyone would expect, but that's exactly what happened to me. Not that most people ever envision finding a dead body at all.

But I, Emily Taylor, was not exactly most people. This sleepy little town was our haven, our sanctuary, to which my husband and I had escaped from a notorious, tragic past.

Not to mention, I was the school principal.

That's why, when I descended those basement stairs of my school that morning, I was more than shocked at the grisly discovery. I felt utterly violated.

I should have known better. I was feeling secure, lulled into a sense of normalcy, life going on at a steady pace. No surprises, kind of dull but satisfying. I marched down those stairs that day with the kind of confidence that comes from usually being in charge, of having control. An assumption that you are safe in a small town, especially in a respected building such as a school.

Although no one could have predicted what I found at the bottom of those stairs, I, of all people, should have known that nothing in this life is definite.

That you can never say never.

CHAPTER 1

The local school was located at the corner of, appropriately, Read and Main Streets, not too far from the canal. The kids went on tours to the locks and made the history and the geography of Burchill very much a part of the curriculum. At least, it had been that way since I became the principal.

Every morning, I jogged up Lakeview to Main, around St. Lawrence to Drummond, and circled back to Read. At first, the villagers were somewhat shocked to see their principal jog to work, but they soon got used to it. I'd always had a weight problem and I was determined to stay fit. Since I wanted to have a quick shower as soon as I arrived, I was always there early, sometimes even before the caretaker, Nathaniel Ryeburn.

Passed by during the industrial era, Burchill remained largely as it was envisioned in the 1890s—a waterside community, quiet tree-lined streets, canal-centered. Walking or jogging down the street was an occasion. You waved, smiled, nodded or talked to everyone. Homes still bore the names of the first families who lived in them and even people who had restored these old houses honoured the original architecture. Most people were in bed at a decent hour, but if you wanted to take a midnight stroll, you always felt safe.

On that particular morning, I spotted Nat's truck in the parking lot as I chugged the rest of the way up Read Street. As I told the police later, there was no other sign of movement. I used the key around my neck to open the door and noted that the alarm had been turned off. Everything was normal. I shifted my backpack to the front, shook out my dress, and headed for the small shower room next to the gym.

Burchill Public School was built nearly thirty years ago, replacing the old school house on Lewis Street, which now served as a bakery and home to one of the local merchants. Due to the fact that the architect worked closely with the principal at that time, it was a cleverly designed building. It even had a convenient, though small, shower for a physical education teacher, if the school had one.

For now, it doubled as my own personal 'beauty' room, where I kept some soap, deodorant, a hair brush, a towel and a little make-up. I didn't use much more than eyeliner and eye shadow. My blond hair was shoulder length with a body perm that allowed a quick brushing after a jog to return it to a lovely shine, turned up a little at the ends. I'd been told that I did not look forty-eight. I thought it was my oval face that gave the illusion of youth. In some social circles, I got obvious looks of approval from other men, or so my husband proudly told me.

After a quick look in the mirror, I headed for the staff room, where Nathaniel always has coffee waiting for me. When I first arrived as principal, I told him not to spoil me like that, but he had given me such a look of disappointment that I allowed the practice to continue. Now and then I made sure to thank him, telling him how much I appreciated that first gulp of caffeine in the morning. His big, innocent face always crinkled in a grin and I was embarrassed to see how much my approval meant to him.

There was no inviting aroma that morning. In fact, the door was locked and the coffee pot was cold and clean, testimony to Nat's absence from the room. Puzzled, I made the coffee myself. While I was waiting for it to drip into the pot, it occurred to me that there was an eerie silence in the building. Normally, there would be the sounds of Nathaniel puttering around, maybe even starting the vacuum cleaner. Without waiting for the rest of the coffee to drip, I headed out into the halls to look for him.

Until then, I hadn't really noticed that a lot of the lights weren't turned on and that many of the doors had been left locked. Nat's usual pattern was to open all the doors first, turning on the hall lights as he went, to make the building bright and inviting for the first teachers to arrive. The outside doors were usually the last to be opened, at about seven-thirty, when one or two of the staff often drifted in. I normally arrived by seven, which was the case that morning. Often Nathaniel got there by 6:30 if he had extra things to do.

Now nearly 7:20, I had still heard no sounds of Nathaniel Ryeburn going about his business. The school was L-shaped, with the office area at the corner of the L, and the staff room and gym at the end of the longer wing. Walking from the staff room, I passed the office, which was dark and locked. I called out at this point, thinking Nathaniel might be in one of the rooms at the other end of the building. As I walked, I opened doors and turned on the hall lights. By now I was a little concerned, even disconcerted. There was something about a deserted building that was unsettling. Especially one that was normally filled with talkative little people. As I rounded the corner, I spotted the open basement door.

Because the school had been built in an era of bomb scares, the architect had designed a basement that could be used by a small number of people. It wasn't clear if he thought that the staff would hide and leave the students to face the bomb, or whether they'd select all the favourites and take them with them, or what he had in mind. In any case, the school had a wonderful storage area right below the short wing of the school. Very few people had been in the basement besides Nathaniel, who was always running up and down the stairs getting supplies. The door, for safety reasons, was absolutely never left open or unlocked.

I poked my head around the open door and was met with semidarkness and silence. The light at the top of the stairs had been turned off, but there seemed to be a dim light somewhere down in the recesses of the basement. Clearing my throat, I called Nat's name twice. No answer. I convinced myself that he must have been down there working on something and couldn't hear me. With that confidence which I was not to feel for a very long time afterward, I descended the stairs.

The steps were rather narrow and steep, which was why the door was supposed to be kept locked at all times. In fact, this was the first time I'd ever seen it ajar. I assumed that Nat hadn't thought it would be a problem leaving it open because it was so early. I crept carefully downward, calling his name as I went.

There was absolutely no answer. The silence felt heavy and ominous. Now I was sure there was something wrong. Maybe Nathaniel had had a heart attack or was hurt and unable to move. He was a very big man, and a twisted ankle could have rendered him helpless. But why doesn't he call out? Is he unconscious?

There was a little electrical room in the corner, where all the wires in the school seemed to gather and multiply. A dim light shone from there and the door stood open. As I walked toward it, I suddenly saw two long legs, clothed in the standard issue blue linen pants that the school board made its caretakers wear. Sprawled on the floor, Nathaniel was completely still, lying in the open doorway.

He's fallen, I thought. He's badly hurt. I'll check and then run for the ambulance. "Nat," I said, softly, concerned.

I was within a couple of feet from him when I saw, in the dim light that left his body in shadow, what was clearly wrong. A gaping hole in the middle of his back had poured a river of blood onto the basement floor all around his hips and waist. I could see a path of brownish red liquid to my left all the way to the door of the electrical room.

Something was clutched in Nathaniel's hand. His head was twisted sideways. His open eyes had once stared at whatever he held. Absurdly, I looked up and noticed the pictures of all of his pets, lovingly placed on the small bulletin board inside the room.

Without thinking, I moved toward Nat and picked up his right arm, which was splayed out toward me. It was cold and clammy. There was no life, no pulse, no sign of the man that had been Nathaniel Ryeburn.

That was when the horror hit me. I straightened up, paralyzed with fear and the sensation that I had been violated, robbed of my security and serenity, bereft and angry and terrified at the same time. While I could only mostly think of myself, the tears began to stream down my face as the loss of this dear man's life slammed past my over developed sense of self preservation. As though peering through a broken camera lens, the scene around me went in and out of focus, zooming in and out, in my numbed head. My heart pounded in my ears and in my mouth. My breath came in clumps. Nausea threatened to overturn the small breakfast I'd had much earlier.

I probably stood there no more than ten seconds, but the shock seemed to last hours. Suddenly I heard a loud banging in the distance and the sound frightened me into action. I raced up the stairs and confronted a face in the side doorway.

CHAPTER 2

Lynda McLeay looked at me quizzically through the window, a fist raised to bang once more on the door. I could tell my face was flushed and my eyes wide with shock and fear. Tears still slid unbidden and unchecked down my cheeks. Lynda froze and simply stared at the sight of her normally composed principal. I opened the door and nearly dragged Lynda inside.

"Lynda, something terrible has happened." My voice croaked and shook. I had to clear my throat to push the words past my lips.

Lynda McLeay was our Grade 8 teacher. She was a big woman, at least six feet tall, probably well over two hundred pounds, with hands that could encircle a small child's waist. Her large, impassive face waited patiently for me to explain. Only her eyes, blinking behind her glasses, showed her surprise.

"Something has happened to Nathaniel. I think he's…I'm sure he's dead."

"Dead? How…?"

"I'm not sure. It looks like he's been shot."

"Oh my God. But…but this is Burchill! We're in a school." Lynda's face was white, almost angry. She felt the violation, too.

"I know. Exactly." Lynda's pinched face and wide eyes were having a calming effect on me. I took both her hands in mine and tried to behave as the principal, the one who always made the tough decisions, the one in charge and in control. I sniffed away the tears and straightened my shoulders.

Taking a deep breath, not planning ahead but thinking as I went, I said, "I'm going to lock the basement door and call Edgar Brennan at the Ontario Provincial Police (OPP) Office. I'll give you my outside door key. Go and unlock the front door. Tell the first person you see about what has happened, and then both of you arrange to meet all staff at the front and side doors. Just let them know there's been an accident. Warn them that an ambulance or a police van may be showing up shortly before bell time and that they are to keep the kids outside and occupied. I want as few people as possible to know about this for now."

Lynda nodded, took the key, and proceeded toward the front door while I locked the basement. For a brief instant I felt as though I were abandoning poor Nat, but then reminded myself that he no longer knew pain or loss. In my office, I began to feel somewhat under control. I was no longer nauseous or dizzy. The shaking had stopped and my voice was steady as I called Edgar Brennan.

I knew that he arrived at the little OPP office on Mill Street at seven every morning, because in the winter, when I walked to work and got there later, I waved at him through the window as I passed by. A quiet, tall, and rather handsome man, Edgar was someone who had the kind of assurance and calm manner that you needed in a police officer.

As soon as I heard his deep, reassuring voice, I felt tears at the back of my eyelids. "Edgar, it's Emily Taylor. I'm calling from the school."

He must have sensed the effort I was making to remain calm, as he was immediately businesslike.

"Edgar, there's been a death at the school. That is, Nathaniel Ryeburn has been shot and—"

He didn't wait for more. "I'll be right there. Have you called Doc Murphy?" When I told him no, he said he'd do that and bring the doctor with him.

After he hung up, I debated about whom to call next. The school board covers a very large area geographically, with the result that the board office is a long way away in a larger city. The school superintendent should certainly be notified, but should I call the local trustee first and have her call the superintendent or vice versa? My thoughts were swirling, getting caught like a flood of water on little bits of flotsam and useless detail. There was nothing in the emergency procedures to cover dead bodies in the basement. In the end, I decided to wait until the Doc and Edgar had looked at the scene.

When I first moved to Burchill, I couldn't believe that the country doctor really did exist. It was like something I'd read about or seen countless times on television or in movies. Doc Murphy was in his fifties. His father was the town doctor before him. There were many rites of passage in Burchill and handing the family business over to your son (or daughter nowadays) was certainly one of them. In the case of the Murphys, Ronald Murphy had left to study in the United States and make his fortune, but had returned when his father suffered a stroke. Ron had never left, even after his father died. Lucky for Burchill, because Ron Murphy was an excellent doctor, one of the best we had ever seen. Like those heart-warming family movies where a village doctor is featured, Ron Murphy was always referred to as 'Doc'.

It wasn't long before I saw Doc and Edgar walking quickly up the sidewalk next to my office window. Keys dangling at my side, I went to the front door to meet them. Lynda stood gravely posted as though she were a Buckingham Palace sentry, her face composed and calm, though her eyes still appeared wide with shock. Edgar and Doc said hello to her, but then moved quickly into the building with me.

"We left our cars down the street, Emily. I don't want the whole town to know what's happening just yet."

"That's great, Ed. The bell will ring in about forty-five minutes and I guess we don't want them greeted with police cars and ambulances."

As we talked, we continued to walk past the office toward the basement door. Doc Murphy put his hand on my shoulder. "This must have been quite a shock, Emily. How do you think it happened?"

"I can't imagine. Maybe he was cleaning his gun or..."

"In the school?" Edgar asked incredulously. "Nat wouldn't be that stupid, would he?"

I just shook my head. Approaching the basement door was making me nervous. My hand shook slightly as I inserted the key and opened it wide enough for Edgar and Doc to pass through. Taking a deep breath, I followed them down the steep steps into the gloom. Edgar stopped us at the bottom of the staircase and, mumbling that he better follow procedure, he asked us to slip on latex gloves.

Doc immediately went to Nat and felt for a pulse, then listened with his stethoscope. "Emily's right, Ed. Nathaniel's gone." He continued carefully feeling around the body, touching Nat's face, searching for answers to questions that I could not even imagine. "He hasn't been dead very long, though. Rigor mortis hasn't progressed very much. It's just hitting the face now. Of course, it's fairly cool down here, but I would say it hasn't been more than…maybe two hours. Could be even less."

Edgar was carefully walking around the body, peering into the electrical room, his perceptive, intelligent eyes taking in every detail. "This might be more serious than I first thought. I was absolutely convinced it was an accident of some kind. Does this look like an accident, Doc?" Ed had followed the trail of blood from the middle of the room. At one point, he stooped over and picked something up from the floor. "Here's where Nat was shot," he said, his voice flat with shock and something that could have been anger. "I believe I just found bullet fragments."

"He must have dragged himself to the electrical room. At that point, he could have been still on his feet." Doc Murphy stood up, puzzled. "What the hell could he have wanted in the electrical room?"

"There's something clutched in his hand," I said, pointing.

Edgar came over and crouched beside Nat. "You're right, Emily, he definitely has something in that hand. It's not the gun, though. Could that be under his body, Doc? Maybe we can carefully lift him a little to see. If it's here, we might be able to safely say that the wound was self-inflicted. Maybe Nat was getting ready to go hunting and was cleaning his gun. If the gun's not here..." He left the rest unsaid, too pained to consider the idea of murder in Burchill.

Once again that overwhelming feeling of violation, of being robbed of my safe haven, threw itself over me like a blanket. I know that I must sound selfish and self-absorbed, and perhaps I was but my past had taught me to be hyper sensitive to threats from the outside. It took very little to awaken the depths of fear and insecurity that I constantly kept at bay. The horror in this room was too much for my tenuous hold on the waves of terror that moved through my nervous system on a daily basis. I had to breathe deeply and steady myself by gripping the banister.

Doc and Edgar carefully lifted Nathaniel until his body was tilted on its side. No gun. "Can we get more light down here, Emily?"

I moved automatically, with each stride regaining control. "I think there's another switch inside the electrical room." I carefully stepped as far as possible around the body, into the small cubbyhole, and searched for the right switch. Nathaniel's pictures of his mother and father and his pets, pinned carefully to the bulletin board, smiled at me as I stood there in the filter of the one dim light bulb. I briefly thought of having to tell Nat's parents, about how lost they would be without him, and I found it difficult to swallow. The Ryeburns were totally dependent on Nat. What would they do now?

As I hit one of the larger switches, the basement was suddenly showered in light. In the glare of reality, the body and the river of blood looked more grotesque, more out-of-place than ever. I was thankful that there were no windows. At least no one from the outside could look in on this ghastly scene. None of the little people, no doubt now milling about in the schoolyard, would be inadvertently exposed to this dreadfulness.

Edgar continued his quiet search, his face wrinkled with thought, anger, and distaste. He had never had to deal with anything like this in his career. Burchill was his birth town. He had never considered the possibility of a murder in this little hamlet. There were occasional skirmishes, even threats, but generally everyone here knew everyone else. They were happy, generous, kind people. Either a stranger had entered their midst, or the appearance of happiness was just that—an appearance.

"Emily, Doc, look carefully for a gun. I can't find one. And if there is no gun, we have to consider the possibility that Nathaniel has been murdered. And that puts everything in an entirely different light. We definitely can't let the children come into the building. Would all the staff be here by now, Emily?"

He talked as he looked, poking into corners, yet careful not to touch or disturb anything. I couldn't move from my position in the electrical room, Nat's pets and his parents peering over my shoulder. Unless Nathaniel had shot himself and then absurdly hidden the gun carefully, there was no weapon in that basement.

I checked my watch. 8:20. "Most of them should be here by now, Ed. The bell rings at 8:45 and we usually have kids in the yard by now, too."

"Okay. I think I'd better call the city. I never even considered the possibility that this would actually be a murder, but I'm afraid that's the only conclusion I can come to now. Shit. I didn't even search the building. The murderer could actually still have been here." Edgar shook his head, feeling and looking the country bumpkin at the moment. "What time did you get here, Emily?"

I shivered. I couldn't help picturing myself showering with carefree security while a murderer lurked in the hallways. Once again I found speech difficult and had to clear my throat several times before I could reply. "At seven. The doors were still locked, but the alarm was turned off, which is normal. I took a shower as I normally did, then I went searching for Nat. I suddenly realized none of the usual doors were unlocked, nor was the coffee made. I saw absolutely no one." I took a deep breath. "It was all dark and quiet and…" To my embarrassment, my voice cracked and the tears spilled over once again.

"It's okay, Emily. Enough for now," Edgar said, his voice soft and comforting. "I'm going to call the city people and get some advice on this. For now, I'd like the staff to stay where they are out in the yard and try to keep the kids busy. Maybe they can gather their classes outdoors. Let them know there's some kind of problem in the school and they can't go in until it's been cleared. I'm also going to call Barry and Mike to do a full search of the building."

Barry Mills and Michael Lewis were two trained volunteers who helped with emergency situations when Edgar was not available. Barry and his wife owned the Main Street Station Pub, famous for its food and hospitality. Michael was a local artist with some national repute.

"I guess I should go over to the Ryeburns' place," Doc said, making the statement a reluctant question.

"Jeez, Doc, I guess so. I'd appreciate that very much. Just tell them as little as possible, okay? They should know Nathaniel's dead, but maybe it's best to be vague about how. They can see the body if they want to, but not 'til he's been moved." Edgar shook his head in disbelief. "I can't get over this. It just doesn't seem possible. I keep hoping I'm dreaming."

In the few seconds that they talked, I was able to gather my inner resources. I am the principal, I told myself. I am in charge, in control, responsible. I spoke up. "I think I'll call a staff meeting, Ed. I can send Lynda and whoever else is standing guard at the doors to round up most of the staff from the yard. Then we can have a plan. Do you think it would be okay to bring them into the gym by the side door? We won't go anywhere else."

"Sounds okay. I guess that would be the best way to keep the kids organized and the parents at bay. Go ahead. Doc and I will take it from here."

I almost raced up the stairs and headed toward the main office. It was now 8:30, so I turned off the bells. Many of our children would be at school by now, playing their innocent games in the yard, secure in the morning sunshine and the protective shadow of the building where they always felt safe and secure. I hated the thought of their peace of mind being shattered, of their assurance threatened, of tearing the net that school should provide for them at all times.

As I was talking to Lynda at the front door, I saw May on the walkway. Lynda and Margaret Johnston, our resource teacher, left their posts at the doors and started rounding up the staff from the yard. May began walking toward me, her hand already outstretched to touch mine, her lovely face suffused with concern, her eyes holding mine steadfastly and openly.

May Reneaux was my age and we were slowly becoming very good friends. Since I had no vice principal, May, as the school secretary, got the first earful of complaints or queries or comments. She was proud of the fact that she could handle any parent without getting ruffled. She could deal with any catastrophe from a bleeding nose, to a lost tooth, to a broken arm. She was articulate, understanding, and dedicated.

May was an attractive woman, a full-blooded Canadian native with dark eyes and long straight hair. She looked slightly overweight, but that was really her sturdy, muscular build draped in the flowing, colourful clothes that she favoured. Her husband, Alain, owned the only full auto service station in town, so they were financially quite well off. May did this job to have some independence and because she truly loved people, big or small. I knew that May would be able to handle this situation, too, probably better than I could.

"What's happened?" she asked calmly, her hand warm and dry and steadying in mine.

Quickly but gently, I pulled her into the hallway and told her. Typically, she was shocked but immediately sensitive to me, clucking sympathetically about how I must be feeling after such a discovery. She enwrapped me in her warm, strong embrace and it was all I could do to prevent myself from pitching forward, staying there forever, rejecting responsibility for the situation, curling up like a child on May's lap, dissolving into and letting all the tears of the past and present enwrap us in a fog of ignorance.

Lynda came into the office just then and informed me that all of the staff had gathered in the gym, save two who remained in the yard to supervise any children who'd already arrived. I stood out of the safety of May's circle, but her strength had infused me with a tonic that waved the uncertainty from my weakened state of mind. I stood up straight once again.

There were thirteen teachers on staff, including myself, the resource teacher, and the French teacher. In my opinion, they were all excellent teachers and wonderful people. Since arriving here at Burchill Public, I had come to appreciate their abilities, their struggles, their quirks, creativity, and skills. I admired their idiosyncrasies as much as their accreditation and knowledge, because their passions and obsessions were what filled them with energy and ideas and love for children. Today I had to count on their professionalism to handle an unprecedented situation, but I had full confidence that they could do it.

The air in the gym was thick with concern, curiosity, even anxiety about this weird twist in their daily routine. The lights hadn't been switched on. The small group stood huddled under a basketball hoop, their faces reddish in the glow of the emergency exit signs. The shadowed atmosphere seemed more than appropriate in the circumstances. I took a huge gulp of air, placing myself in the middle of the circle, and began.

"I know you've been told there's been a terrible accident. It's actually worse than that. Nathaniel has been shot and killed." I waited for the gasps and whispers to subside. "We have no idea how this could have happened, but it looks like someone—it looks like it was deliberate." I couldn't say it, but the word 'murder' echoed on their faces and in their eyes. "I realize that this is a horrible shock for you. It is for me, too, and I hate so much to burden you with it. But right now we have to somehow submerge our feelings and our questions and deal with the kids first. When I've got all the information, we'll discuss everything."

"Edgar Brennan is here and Doc Murphy just left. Ed wants us to keep the kids outside until he gets advice from the OPP in Ottawa. We don't know if they'll want to close the school or what the decision might be. It depends on the results of their investigation, I guess. Barry and Mike will be arriving soon to help."

"It might be a good idea to get the kids together somewhere in the yard in your class groupings first, take attendance and let them know there's some kind of problem in the building. Don't let on that you know any details at all. If any parents of your own students bring the kids into the yard, you can let them know they can take them right back home if they want to. Just keep a notation of who has come and gone. After that, if we're still outside, I guess you'll have to keep them entertained somehow." I knew I was rambling, but they held fast to each word, saying absolutely nothing, only the sounds of expelled breath and small exclamations squeezed between my sentences.

"Why don't I lead them in the songs we're doing for the school concert?" Margaret Johnston, resource teacher, piano player, concert organizer, and, I thought at that moment, all-round wonderful woman, offered, her voice sounding loud and firm in the silence.

Everyone nodded. They began to murmur with determination, agreeing that they would have no problem keeping the kids entertained. The children were, after all, the priority, as always. I thanked them profusely for being so calm and professional as they went back out the gym doors and into the gathering groups of little ones in the yard. Once again, I blessed the principal before me, who had interviewed and hired this amazing group of people, and then had persuaded them to stay, despite the fact that an interloper was coming to town to take over when he retired. In the two years that I'd been here, I thought I'd done a good job establishing a rapport with the staff and the community. I was going to need to lean on that under these circumstances.

When I returned to my office, Edgar was waiting with the door open. He waved me in, his face grave.

"The city people will be down here in half an hour. They advise that we get on the phone right now and begin telling parents to come and pick up their children. Good thing it's Friday. At least we'll have the weekend to finish any investigating that has to be done and then a decision can be made about allowing the kids back into the building." Edgar ran his hand through his hair, his face filled with sorrow. "I can't believe this. Who the hell would want to kill Nathaniel Ryeburn? Especially here, right in the school..."

Who indeed? If only I had been able to look into the future, I would have seen that there are actually even worse things than the desecration of a school building.

CHAPTER 3

I couldn't answer Edgar's lament. I had to distance myself from the horror. I had to be objective and logical. I had to remember that everyone was depending on me.

Right now I was trying to focus my mind on the emergency system that we have in place for sending the kids home. Every parent must fill out a card that dictated to where and with whom the students were dismissed if the school was closed because of weather or some other emergency. Like Edgar, I still couldn't comprehend the emergency we had just encountered.

As soon as I had asked May to round up all the emergency cards, I waved Paul Granmercy, the French teacher, and Diane West, the Kindergarten assistant, back into the school. Before the three of them began the tedious task of calling every parent of three hundred and sixteen students—a total of one hundred and twelve families—I placed calls to the school board and the local trustee. It was not an easy task. Both the trustee and the superintendent of schools insisted that they would be right over.

Despite numerous questions as May, Paul and Diane began their calls to the families, they continued to tell the parents that it was an emergency within the school building itself and that they had no details. They were also instructed to say—just like in the movies—that: "Mrs. Taylor is unavailable for comment". I knew I simply couldn't handle that right now. Besides, I had no idea what I could say. Let them believe it was something to do with the building. Allow them a little more time of peace and innocence and security.

Meanwhile, Edgar had moved his OPP car to the front of the school. Mike and Barry arrived shortly after the phone calls to parents began, so Edgar placed Barry at the front door to direct them to the yard to collect their children (and deflect any of the curious). It was an excellent choice, for Barry was extremely popular and respected throughout Burchill. He was a tall, slightly overweight, redheaded man with a huge laugh and an intimate handshake. From his experience in running the local pub and restaurant, he was skilled with people in all kinds of situations. He handled the parents, who began almost immediately to arrive at the school, with diplomacy and reassurance.

On the other hand, Michael Lewis was a small, bespectacled, sandy-haired man with the fine, delicate hands of an artist. He also had the mathematician's attention to detail that was required when you drew a complex scene and then added colour. He was the perfect companion for Edgar and me as we prowled the school looking for anything out of the ordinary. Answering Mike's numerous questions kept me occupied and alert. I was able to forget the fatigue that sometimes accompanies shock and nervousness.

In the midst of parents arriving and toward the end of our school tour, the team from Ottawa, the school board Superintendent, and the local Trustee all descended upon the scene at once. The OPP officers arrived in two marked cars, two unmarked cars, a coroner's station wagon, and an emergency vehicle. The entire front yard was filled with vehicles. That should rouse the parents, I thought, as Mike Lewis went out to join Barry in directing the confused mothers, fathers, or baby-sitters to the back yard.

At first it was chaos as the Ottawa people and the school board officials jockeyed for power. A short, stout man with a beard, Peter McGraw belonged in the fairly isolated school board office. He was organized, knew all the rules, regulations and memoranda, but was completely without people skills. Connie Cicero, the Trustee, was pretty well ignorant of the rules and regs, but she could collect anyone's vote with her dazzling smile and empathetic blue eyes.

I had never met any of the Ottawa police before. In the confusion, I simply had an impression of big—big men, mostly, in uniform or suit, some with equipment, all quiet and hovering, except for one who immediately began asking questions.

In the end, it was Edgar who assumed command. He did it by first introducing everyone with our names and position, thereby establishing our roles. Next he informed Peter and Connie that the 'accident scene' was no place for anyone but the trained experts and he was 'certain that

Emily did not want to go back down there'. He suggested, nicely but firmly, that they stay with me to review what the school personnel had done so far and to plan strategy for what must be done next. The Ottawa team fanned out from there, most toward the basement, some to inspect the rest of the building. At that point, Edgar deferred to Constable Ducek, the man with all the questions, murmuring answers as they proceeded down the hall.

    I took Connie and Peter into my office where we all had coffee first, clucking over the incredulous occurrence. Once we got to work, our team turned out to be quite compatible. Peter, with his knowledge of the rules, was able to guide us through the proper procedures that the board and the parents should be able to expect. Connie, concerned with appearances and public relations, gave solid advice about how to handle the press and the parental reaction. My concern was the emotional stability of both the children and the staff. Eventually, we were able to put together a step-by-step plan that included calling the *Burchill Banner*, sending home a carefully worded letter, and calling on the services of a trained psychologist and child and youth worker from the main board office. When we were finished, and Connie and Peter gone, I actually felt much better.

    By the time we emerged from the meeting, most of the parents and students had dispersed. The staff had been permitted to take the few remaining children into the gym out of the quickly heating sun. Teachers were taking turns entertaining them. The rest of them were sitting in pairs or groups of three whispering to one another. There was a shocked quietness about their movements. They still couldn't believe this was happening in their little town, and the thought of Nathaniel lying dead in the basement was beyond imagination.

    I hadn't flashed back to that scene during the meeting with Peter and Connie. Now, in their wake, images of blood, Nat's sprawled and lifeless body, his clenched fist and staring eyes, kept darting through my thoughts like a film on ultra speed, startling me every time with their clarity and their power.

    I knew I had to keep busy. I checked with May and found that six families couldn't be reached for various reasons. She was working on emergency alternatives. Barry and Mike had left, Barry to the restaurant to prepare for the day, Mike to answer any calls that came to the OPP office. I found Edgar near the basement door, talking to some of the Ottawa team. His face opened up with concern when he saw me.

    "Emily! I see the kids have mostly been sent home. How did the parents take it? How was your meeting with Peter and Connie? How's the staff holding up?"

I smiled at his unusual verbosity. "The meeting actually went better than I expected. Peter and Connie were really helpful and I think we have a sensible plan in place. Barry and Mike were great with the parents. They're confused, but Connie's on her way to the *Banner* to file a well-worded report for this afternoon's paper, so that should help. It's vague enough but truthful enough to keep parents calm, I hope. The staff's still waiting in the gym. I just came to ask you if we should be doing anything else at this point. Also, do you think they can go to the staff room? I'd like to fortify them with some coffee if I can and it's right across from the gym. They could take turns."

The OPP officer from Ottawa answered at Edgar's gesture of inquiry in his direction. "Sure, let them get some coffee and a little fortification. I'll send an officer down there to supervise. We'll need to question all of the staff members, especially you, Mrs. Taylor. After that, we can start letting people go home. We'll start in about fifteen minutes. Okay?"

"Sure, no problem. Since this is the weekend, we won't need a further closing of the school, will we?"

"I don't see any reason to do that at this point. We may need to reassure parents that their kids are in no danger, that this is an isolated incident, etc."

"The newspaper article we composed does that well, I think. We're also planning to send a letter home with the kids on Monday to reinforce that. We might even figure out a way to deliver them on Sunday."

"Let's talk about all of this a little later. I'll fill you in on the investigation. I think you need more information than the rest of the population." The officer smiled at me and turned back to the basement door.

I went to my office and shut the door. It was time to call my husband. Langford Taylor was a prominent artist in Ontario. He painted watercolours mostly, of scenes in and around Burchill. He'd been compared to Tom Thomson and some of the *Group of Seven* and in fact, made a pretty good wage these days from his talent. Few people know that his first name was actually William. For me, 'Will' had become an endearment, one I used only when we were alone, a reminder of a time when we were so close yet so far apart. I thought he might be out in the studio, but he answered the telephone right away. As soon as I heard his voice, my composure left me and I began to cry.

"Em, what's wrong? What is it, honey? Should I come over?"

I managed to choke down the sobs then. "No, no, for god's sake, don't do that, Will. I have to look like I'm handling this." I gave a short, unamused laugh and dabbed at my nose and eyes with a tissue, trying to stem the current of feeling that was leaking out of me. "Honey, something terrible has happened at the school. Nathaniel Ryeburn has been murdered. I found his body in the basement."

He was silent for a moment, digesting the information. "What? Oh my god. Emily, this is incredible." His voice held all the emotion that I felt—the violation, the fear, the disbelief that murder had followed us to this little haven. I was in danger of dissolving into tears again.

"The OPP from Ottawa are here investigating. Edgar's been great and so have the staff. I'm just waiting to be questioned." Again, that shaky laugh betrayed my nervousness and fear. Was our life about to change again?

"Emily, don't worry. There's no connection between this and Vancouver. Don't be afraid, darling. It's going to be all right. Are you sure you don't want me to come up there?"

"I'm sure. I really will be okay. And, Will, I never thought there was a connection to *you*. It's just that Burchill is our sanctuary..." To my chagrin, my voice broke a bit again.

"I didn't mean that you would think there was a connection with me," Will said almost angrily. "I just meant...it's not the end of our life here."

He was always reading my thoughts. But right now communication wasn't the best. We were in danger of isolating one another, and I knew it. I needed to be face to face, to touch his hands, to look into his eyes. This is the man I have loved for more than twenty-five years and I knew better than to short-change this conversation by submerging any of the feelings that we would have to deal with in the next few days. It was a conversation for home, for the lake, for the swing on the porch.

"I know it won't be," I said, trying to sound as though I had conviction, determined to have the strength to get through the rest of the day. "I love you, Will."

"I love you, too, Em. Will you be sent home early?"

"I think so. All the kids are gone now. I'm sure the staff and I will be next, after they question us..." My voice stuck on the word, the questioning, the relentless asking, the flashing of camera bulbs, the...My husband's words brought me back to the present, to Burchill, to here, in this school of this little town, where I was in control.

"If I'm not here, I'll be in the studio. I've got to finish some of *Silver Lake* before I lose the inspiration or the light, whichever comes first." He laughed softly.

"Get to work, then. I'll probably see you early this afternoon." We said good-bye, almost as if this were a normal day, and hung up. For a few minutes, I could do nothing but stare at the telephone, thinking nothing and everything at once. Images flashed through my mind without thought or logic. My heart pounded heavily. I couldn't help myself. I was afraid.

CHAPTER 4

A knock at the door cleared my head at once. Guiltily, as if I'd been derelict in my duties, I leaped up and threw open the door.

Edgar stood there, almost apologetically. "Constables Ducek and Petapiece want to start the interviews with you. Then they'll just ask the staff a few questions about when they arrived, where they live, stuff like that, and then everyone can go home. I think they've been under enough stress. They need to get back to their own children, their own families."

"Would my office be the best place for the interviews?" I asked, appreciating for the umpteenth time the soft colours, the large curtained window, the comfortable chairs, the large desk.

"Sure. I'll get Ducek and Petapiece in here now. Do you want me to stay?"

"Definitely."

Constable Ducek arrived with a younger female officer, presumably Petapiece, and several note pads. He sat at my desk, while the rest of us spread out in the chairs. "Okay, Mrs. Taylor, just lead us through your steps this morning."

I told them about my morning routine, about arriving at seven. I felt my face flush at the thought of taking my usual quick shower while poor Nat lay bleeding downstairs. Then I retraced my thought process as it led me to the basement stairs. I described as dispassionately as possible the scene that I had come upon, talked about the blood, about touching Nat's wrist to feel for a pulse, pretending it was a story I was telling about someone else.

There is something about speaking from the principal's chair that infuses authority. I was far calmer and more in possession of my faculties than I'd been all morning. "He didn't even feel warm to the touch," I said, still feeling the surprise and shock, but becoming more objective as I remembered to whom I was speaking. "But it's funny, because Nat doesn't usually get here until six thirty or seven himself."

Constable Petapiece spoke. "It looks like Mr. Ryeburn had been dead over an hour when you arrived. The coroner can't determine that for sure until there's an autopsy, but Dr. Ogilvy is uncannily accurate, and his opinion is backed up by Burchill's own doctor."

"So Nat must've come here really early. That's very unusual." I began to picture him, lumbering through the dusky hallways, making his way to the basement in half-light. Why? "What was clenched in his hand?" I knew they were supposed to be asking the questions, but I needed to know.

The Constables glanced at one another. "It was a picture of his mother and father and his pets," Constable Ducek said, the tone of his voice displaying a mixture of pity and curiosity.

I nodded my head. "I'm not surprised. Nat is very devoted to his parents and the animals that he cares for. His place is like a small zoo. Any hurt or stray animal is immediately taken to Nathaniel to be looked after. It doesn't please our local vet." Then it flashed into my mind that the situation would be different from now on and I felt my face colour in shame at having smiled.

"I need to know one more thing, and then I'll be quiet. Could I have...if I hadn't come in and spent time in the shower and making coffee and opening doors...could I have saved him?" I tried my best to hold my head up, to perfect that icy principal's stare, in order to avoid having my voice break and losing my dignity.

Constable Ducek looked at me thoughtfully, directly into my eyes. The clench of my fingers must have belied the feelings behind the question. I had to look away before tears came. "No, Mrs. Taylor, it doesn't look that way. Mr. Ryeburn was shot with a 30.30 calibre rifle, with a soft-nosed hunting bullet. Unfortunately, that meant almost instant death for the poor guy. He caught it in the stomach area, so he lived maybe fifteen minutes, probably in agony, only long enough to stagger to the electrical room and grab that picture. I can't imagine what was going on in his mind at that moment. But no, Emily," his use of my first name was meant to be comforting, "you couldn't have saved him. He was dead when you arrived at the school."

My mind drew back to my arrival (was it only four hours ago?) and the thought of casually going about my regular routine with Nathaniel's body so close by made me shiver. I doubted that I'd ever again feel so secure and safe in my own school.

After a few more perfunctory questions, I was dismissed, and the officers began their short interviews with the staff. As each meeting concluded, the teachers were sent to the sanctuary of their homes. I waited, with May for support, until everyone was gone. In the meantime, almost surreptitiously, the Ottawa team removed Nathaniel's body, whisking it away in the coroner's hearse. I stood at the window of my office and watched, wondering, not for the last time, who on earth would have wanted to kill Nathaniel Ryeburn, one of the mildest, sweetest men I'd ever met.

"I'll call you later," May had said, and then she waved at me as she traced her steps back along the walkway, her face crumpled with concern, her eyes holding onto mine for as long as she could before she straightened and headed for home.

The Ottawa team was still investigating, hidden in the depths of the basement, when they released me. They knew 'where to find me,' Edgar told me, squeezing my hand for reassurance, so I could go home for now. He couldn't know how those words affected me. Edgar couldn't hear the echoes of my past that made this particular expression so threatening. Where he thought he was being funny, and therefore supportive, he had chosen words that caused those waves to begin crashing once more against clumsily piled rocks that form my wall of security, control, peace, hope.

CHAPTER 5

The weather hadn't cooperated in reflecting the horror of this day. It was beautiful—sunny, dry and breezy. Friendly white clouds drifted in the light blue sky. I walked quickly, afraid that at any moment a parent would come up and start questioning me. I kept hearing those words, so innocent and yet so ominous: *we know where to find you.* For a moment I almost wished we were living in a big, anonymous city, but then I reminded myself that even there, they had known where to find us. I don't remember much about that walk home, except that as I passed close to the Ryeburns' residence, I thought that I should go in and see the old couple, but couldn't force my feet in their direction. There was nothing I could do until I had felt Will's arms around me.

My husband and I lived in what was known as the 'Beatty House'. A turn of the century frame house, it was lovingly restored by the couple who lived there before us. It had two beautiful verandas at both the front and back doors. The back porch had been screened in and enlarged. Best of all, it overlooked Ogeechee Lake and was surrounded by lovely old trees. We were right at the end of the street, which was, naturally, called Lakeview Road. The house was painted a light blue with white shutters, looking somewhat Cape Cod-ish. It had been modernized just enough to suit a professional couple's tastes, but not enough to spoil its original grandeur. Though listed in the 'Walking Tour' book sold to tourists, it was too far from the main street for most people to bother coming by.

I cannot tell you how stunned I was when I first saw Beatty House. It was as though someone reached into my dreams and built the one place in which I would feel completely, totally, at home. I loved it then and I loved it now, two years later.

What I pictured in my mind as I walked home that day was the front porch surrounded by the purple flowers that I've never learned the names of, lovingly planted there by Will. I imagined the front door with the brown straw bonnet welcome sign, its bright silk buds around the rim, and the curtains, which trim the windows so perfectly. I saw the living room, the comfortable chairs, the stereo in front of which Will and I spend so many nights just listening.

And as I walked, the distance seemed to grow longer, the house further away, and my heart pounded with panic. I saw him through the glass of a prison meeting room, through the bars of the prison doors, through the cement of the prison walls. It seemed that I would never reach him, never feel his arms around me. I walked faster, my back ramrod straight, my eyes unblinking behind the sunglasses, feeling as if I were starring in a bad horror movie.

I caught a glimpse of Will watching for me from the studio window. Half his mind still lay with *Silver Lake,* I could tell. The other half of his consciousness was suddenly with me, probably wondering when I'd come around the corner of the house. When he saw me, I was walking swiftly, almost running. I was certain he could feel my panic from here. No one else would have been able to tell. Only he would know that within the straight-backed posture, the purposeful stride, lay panic and distress underneath. The rest of the world would see a not unattractive, slim blond, every hair in place, dress unwrinkled despite the long hot day, shoes sensible but fashionable. The local school principal—in control, a friendly enough person who was firm, capable and efficient.

By the time Will opened the studio door, I was there, my eyes full, stumbling into his arms. He drew me inside and held me while I trembled and cried, sobs that had everything to do with Nathaniel Ryeburn and the discovery this morning, and yet had nothing to do with that at all. When I was calm, we went into the house and sat in the kitchen.

The three-quarter length windows looked out past the birch trees and tall spindly oaks to the blue of the lake. The calm surface of the water never failed to lull me, rocking me into a sense of peace and happiness that I would never take for granted.

Will made lunch while I talked, telling him every detail. At the tale of the picture clutched in Nathaniel's hand, Will stopped me. "Isn't that strange, Em? I mean, the guy's in agony and all he can think of..."

"Not if you knew Nathaniel." I took a cracker and a piece of cheese from the plate he held out to me. "He's just so dedicated to his parents and to those pets of his. He takes—took—such good care of them all. I don't know what the Ryeburns will do without him."

"I've seen old Mr. Ryeburn a few times out by the locks." Will leaned over the counter and sipped his lemonade. "He looks in pretty good shape for a man his age. He and Nat could've been twins."

"I think he's had a heart attack, but seems to be in fairly good health right now. From what I can gather, he just has to take it easy. God, imagine what the stress of this might do to him."

"I don't think I've ever seen Mrs. Ryeburn. Is she sickly?"

"She's pretty much confined to a wheelchair. Nat brings her to church now and then... I keep talking about him as if he's still here. I've never heard her speak a word, even when spoken to. Some of the townspeople have said that she was always mean-spirited, even before she was ill." I tapped my glass pensively. "They were a town mystery, even before this happened."

"Really?" He sat on the stool beside me. I could feel the warmth of his body, the intensity of his attention. Langford had an unerring quality of what I called deep listening that could unnerve people who didn't know him. His propensity for leaning toward the speaker, head on a slight tilt, towering over them, his eyes direct and carefully scrutinizing, could be intimidating. But it was this spotlight of care and concentration that also endeared him to those who knew him well. For me, I sensed that I was beginning to return to a semblance of normality, buoyed by his support, even as my mind rejected the absurd events of the day.

"Yah. One of our parents, Ruth McEntyer—she seems to know everything—once told me that there are all kinds of strange rumours about the Ryeburns. Walter was reportedly a wild man. Mrs. Ryeburn was a town beauty who all but disappeared into the house when she married him. Ruth seemed to suggest that Annie and Nathaniel were prisoners of sorts."

"Obviously, you doubt her word."

I looked over at him, smiling, hearing the patience in his voice. I took a moment to study him, his dark hair shot with silver, his brown eyes crinkled in interest, the curve of his lips, his strong fingers curled around the glass. I knew he was encouraging my thought process, knew it was the beginning of healing. I never tired of him, looking at him, touching him. I would always appreciate his nearness, I thought, remembering the times when I hadn't been free to reach out for him.

"It just seems to me that if you really want to get out of something, you could in this day and age. Nathaniel did leave town for some time after he'd finished high school. And it was during this time that Mr. Ryeburn had a heart attack and Mrs. Ryeburn got whatever it is that put her in the wheelchair. They just didn't seem able to function without him. Then suddenly one day Nat arrived back home, as quietly as he'd left. No one dared ask where he'd been. They just talked about it behind his back—still do in fact. He immediately stepped into his father's shoes and resumed taking care of them. Plus he took on the caretaker's job at the school."

Will traced the delicate hairs along my fingers. "Do you think Walter and Nathaniel could've had a huge row? Maybe Nat was shot accidentally in the process."

I shivered. "That sounds so abhorrent, but I guess you never know." I gazed out at the lake, watched as a seagull dipped its beak below the surface. I followed a gentle wave as it lapped against our dock. I love this house, this lake, this town. I wondered if it would be the same from now on, or if this experience would always darken my thoughts. "Will, I asked the Constables from Ottawa if they thought I could have saved Nat. I mean, I followed my regular routine, showered, even started making coffee, and there was the poor guy, dying in the basement…" A shiver ran through me, prompting Will to pull his chair close, put his arms around me.

"And they assured you there was nothing you could have done, right?"

I looked up at him, my eyes filled with tears. "Yes, but I still feel weird. I mean, there I was…"

"Completely innocent," Will interjected. "It looks and sounds weird to be following some regular routine when a tragedy is occurring right before you. But remember, if no one had killed poor Nathaniel, your routine would have made perfect sense."

His words brought me back to another time when a sensible routine had been made to seem sinister. 'I'm not even a suspect', and the words, 'We know where to find you', even though they were spoken innocently, even kindly, were really unsettling. I can't imagine how…

Will removed his arms and snatched up the dishes, cutting me off with the movement. I recognized his need to disconnect and honoured it by remaining silent, by pulling back to the present, by forcing my thoughts to be distant and logical. It was a technique that I had not quite perfected, because it went against my innate nature to deal with things openly, immediately, emotionally.

"Would you like to lie down for a while, Em? In case you haven't noticed, I unplugged all the phones except for the one upstairs, which I connected to the answering machine. I can just imagine the calls you're getting and are going to get. Feel like sleeping or talking to people?"

I tapped my glass, considering. I wasn't sure if I could face the darkness of sleep just yet, but didn't know if I wanted to talk to irate or upset parents either. "I think I'll talk, at least for a while. Depending on the reactions I get, I might be able to talk for a long time—or maybe I'll just be able to handle a little. At least I know what to say now that our newspaper item has been hashed out. We're just giving the bare facts for now, letting them know an investigation is taking place and we can't really talk too much about it. Protect the children, stifle curiosity if you can, blah blah blah. By the way, how's *Silver Lake*?"

"A few finishing touches, and I'm done."

I hugged him. "How about if I talk on the phone and you put those finishing touches on the *Lake*? Then do you think I should go and see the Ryeburns?"

"I think it would be perfectly acceptable if you waited until morning, Em. You've been through a lot. I'll go with you."

We decided to go to the Ryeburns' around ten the next morning. While Langford Taylor headed out to his studio, I climbed the steps to our bedroom, suddenly tired, my legs aching with the sudden release of tension. Standing in the doorway, I drew in a breath of strength, drawing from the sunlight as it made silhouettes of our furniture, the quilt, the curtains, Will's pictures. This was my favourite room, the main reason I had told Will that this was the house we'd live in forever.

A huge room, it ran the entire length of the house and had been modernized with the addition of a small en suite bathroom and a walk-in closet. Our four-poster bed, the exact kind I'd dreamed of for years, stood near the bay windows, the curtains gently blowing inward. When I lay down, I could hear the waves lapping at the rocks, smell the scent of the woods and the deep fresh water. From the bedroom, I could step out onto a balcony that was almost a duplicate of the porch below. Here I was able to revel in every season, in the lush green of spring, the bustle of summer, the iridescent colours of autumn, the pristine white of winter. I had always felt that some part of my soul had been missing, until I came to this house in Burchill. Now it seemed that I was complete, that my body and mind had blended with the lake, with the peace of this house, with Will's presence.

The blinking light of the answering machine in the den was like a warning, a siren, a shattering of that fragile tranquility. For a moment, I thought I wouldn't have the strength to listen, to cope. But once I began to play back the messages—the plaintive voices of the parents, the inquisitive tone of a reporter from Ottawa—my resolve returned and I began to return some of the calls. An hour later, Will found me there still speaking calmly, reassuring others, with a strength and conviction I didn't always feel.

He began to rub my neck, kneading the tension in my shoulders, letting his hands play over the small soft hairs at the nape of my neck. Standing very close to me, touching me, I could feel his body begin to respond, as I snuggled into his arms. I turned as I finished the last call, my arms around his hips, my face buried in his t-shirt. I loved the smell of him, slightly sweaty mixed with a little of the fragrance of paint and soap. He tilted my head up, smiled at me, his eyes tracing over my face with the gratitude and wonder of someone who had almost lost his love and would forever appreciate regaining it.

We kissed for a while, slowly at first and then more urgently, before he led me to our bed. Once we were undressed, he caressed me, his artist's hands exploring my body with tenderness and knowledge. I allowed my mind to drift, became aware only of the soft hairs of his body, the gentleness of his fingers, the wetness of my response. When he was inside me, I let myself blend into him, felt the strength flowing between us, knew that whatever else happened in our lives, this was all that was really important.

Later he held me close, while I slept, the images of the day crowding through my mind, the questions, the voices, the image of Nathaniel and the picture clutched in his hand. When I awoke the next morning, I actually felt refreshed, still flushed with love and the confidence that comes from knowing you're truly loved in return. It was with this certainty that I set out with Will to see the Ryeburns.

CHAPTER 6

An outrageous river tumbled through Burchill, bursting into a beautiful little falls that hit the town with enough power to run a woollen mill. There was a canal and a system of locks that by-passed the wildest sections of Kanawhe River. All along the canal, picnic benches dotted the lush green grass, tucked under the shade of huge, ancient sugar maples, oaks and evergreen trees.

In the summer the town was inundated with tourists. They gathered at the locks, fascinated by the parade of yachts and pleasure craft. Many of the seafarers joined the residents for a day or a week at a time. No one in the village minded. In fact, several fancy shops and restaurants had sprung up and people made a good living from the tourist industry.

The lockmaster's house was built by the Ryeburns' ancestors in the early 1800's, when most traffic came by way of the lakes and rivers, and the first canal had been built. It was a small house, built of limestone and timber, designed only to house the lockmaster and his family. Very little had been done to change it, except for the huge wooden fence that encircled the large backyard.

Here Nathaniel Ryeburn kept his beloved pets, acting as refuge provider for any stray or abandoned animal.

From the small, closely cropped lawn, it was only steps to the canal and the lock, which was now mostly electronic. Nat had trained many college students over the years to run the locks in the summer, when the pleasure craft traffic was heavy. He and his father had become overseers on a job that used to consume all their ancestors' time. Across the canal were the lawns of the provincial park, dark green and manicured, and beyond, the lake could be seen with its startling blue and white waves. Although I could not imagine anyone other than the Ryeburns living there, the view alone would attract any admirer of older homes.

Will knocked at the thick wooden door and the echo could be heard in the hallway. For a few moments I thought they wouldn't answer, and I was almost glad at the idea of turning around and heading for home. This was not something I was looking forward to. Then suddenly the door opened and Walter Ryeburn stood framed in the darkness of the hall behind him.

"I told you, I ain't giving no interviews." He leaned a little into the sun, where Will and I could see the puffiness of his eyes as he glared in anger at the shadowed figures in his doorway. His big hands, spotted with age and hard work, clutched the doorframe as if he were ready to hurl himself at us should we come any closer.

"Mr. Ryeburn, it's Emily Taylor. The school principal." When there was no response, I added, deliberately past tense, "I worked with Nathaniel."

The old man grunted, leaning further into the sunlight in order to see his visitors more clearly. "Eh?" Studying my face, his eyes became less pinched, almost friendly. "Oh, yeah, he likes you. He says you're good to him." The latter was said with cynical surprise.

"I just wanted to tell you and Mrs. Ryeburn how sorry I am. I really like Nathaniel and he's—he was a wonderful person to work with."

"I think the missus would like to hear that. Come in." He opened the door into a huge hallway, cavernous because of the twelve-foot ceiling and the grey, nondescript walls. Walter Ryeburn, despite his six-foot frame, seemed dwarfed in the semidarkness. As we followed him, I noticed that his shoulders were rounded. He was stooped and old, no longer 'in good shape for a man his age'. What was the death of his only son going to do to him as the reality of it began to last day after day?

He led us into a huge room filled with sofas and chairs, tables and rugs, an ancient television set, and several cats. Despite the partitions and the carpets, it still looked like an old, converted warehouse. In fact, the air in the room was musty and damp. The windows were small, and behind the curtains, only a little of the afternoon sun filtered in.

"Have a seat. I'll get the missus."

I caught Will's eye, as we gingerly sat on the edge of one of the sofas, squeezing his hand for reassurance. His look told me that he was wondering the same thing. What would it have been like to grow up in a house like this?

"Nat must have thought a lot of you for his father to let you in," Will whispered in my ear. "It doesn't look like they've had visitors since the war." My look warned him to be quiet, but I couldn't help grinning at him.

We heard her voice first, high and querulous, echoing from somewhere in the darkness. Suddenly she appeared in the doorway, an apparition in white, Walter right behind her, carefully manoeuvring the wheelchair past the furniture.

Annie Ryeburn's hair flowed long and thin over her shoulders, almost matching the paleness of her face. Her veined, trembling hands flitted over her nightgown, smoothing and pulling, tugging over her long legs, despite the fact that it almost reached the ground. It was a thin gown, and I, embarrassed, could see the woman's pale, almost bluish, skin through the material. Confused, I looked up at Walter's face, wondering why he would allow such an intrusion. His eyes crinkled at me in a friendly smile, seemingly oblivious to the discomfort in the room.

I got up and went forward, sympathy and pity propelling me to the woman's side. I grasped the thin, cold hands in mine and leaned over to look into her face. I met fear, anger and strength in those blue eyes, not confusion or weakness. I felt as though Annie Ryeburn were trying to give me a message in that icy stare.

"I'm so sorry about Nathaniel, Mrs. Ryeburn. I cared for him very much. He was always there to help me." To my surprise, I felt tears slip down my cheeks. I had to bite my lip to keep from dissolving into weeping.

Mrs. Ryeburn's glare softened. A look of pain crossed her features that deepened the wrinkles and made her look even older. When she spoke, her voice was shaky and high-pitched. "Thank-you, Mrs. Taylor. Nathaniel thought very highly of you. It was nice of you to stop by with your sympathy. You as well, Mr. Taylor. Nat always enjoyed your paintings." With those words, she was suddenly a dignified lady. Her proud head nodded to dismiss us. We quickly gave our good-byes and let ourselves out of the musty hallway.

We ran-walked to the bridge, hand-in-hand, saying nothing until we had reached the other side of the canal.

"How the hell could he do that to her, and why?"

"She was so embarrassed—you could see right through that gown. Do you think he realized...?"

Will nodded his head angrily. "I do, Em. She's so thin and light, he probably picked her right up out of her bed and stuck her in the wheelchair. The only question in my mind is why he would do that."

"I've never really seen them together. As I told you, Nat sometimes brought her to church, but I've never actually seen Mr. and Mrs. in the same room together. Maybe they actually hate one another and Nat was all that kept them from disintegrating totally. Maybe he really did keep her a prisoner in her own home, abused her, whatever. I wonder what will happen now."

As we approached Rideau Street, children could be seen playing on the swings and slides in the park. To me, it appeared as though their parents hovered even closer today. We met Timmy McEntyer and his mother, Ruth, at the top of the incline. "I'm so shocked to hear about Nat," she said immediately. "It must have been awful for you, finding him like that, Mrs. Taylor. To have something like that happen in the basement of our own little school—unbelievable."

I nodded. "It certainly is. I'm very shocked, too." I thought, but of course didn't say, that I was shocked at her level of knowledge and wondered how many of the details she really did know.

"Nat was such an amazing man. People are going to miss talking to him."

Confused, I repeated, "Talking to him?", even as I pictured Nathaniel, stoic and silent, washing the floor or changing a light bulb, smiling with his eyes lowered, bringing me coffee without ever looking me directly in the face.

"Oh, yes, didn't you know? The bridgeman was practically the town counsellor." She turned quickly as she spotted Timmy racing toward the swings. "Well, I'd better go. I guess we'll all be gathering at the funeral...." Waving, her words disappearing as she walked away, Ruth McEntyer followed her child into the park.

Will and I gazed at each other, the bewilderment in his eyes reflecting my own reaction. "I guess there's a lot about Nathaniel Ryeburn that I never knew," I said. I had no idea how understated my words would seem to me later.

By Saturday evening, the town was full of reporters, including a couple of television camera crews. June had been a slow month for news, it seemed, and the sensation of a body in the basement of a school was something for the front pages of the *Ottawa Examiner* and even the *Toronto Gazette*, as well as several seconds of televised news time.

Word quickly spread around town that the Ryeburns were in deep shock and should be left alone. Despite the Ryeburns' odd home life and taciturn attitudes toward the townspeople, no one seemed tempted to allow the rest of the world into their lives. After all, the Ryeburns had been the bridgemen for longer than anyone could remember. The villagers gathered like protective clothing over the former bridgeman and his wife.

At the Main Street Station Pub, Barry Mills distracted the reporters by telling them that he had been "practically first on the scene" and letting them know that the Ryeburns had "gone into seclusion and were not at home". Bill and Marjory Percival and their sons booked everyone into the Burchill Inn and then sent them on expeditions into the countryside looking for the Ryeburns' 'retreat'.

"By the time they figure out there's no retreat," Bill was heard to chuckle, "poor Nat'll be put to rest."

It was more than protecting someone whose history was entwined with theirs, I was to discover. Nathaniel Ryeburn had certainly been the popular man that Ruth McEntyer had described to us. The townspeople genuinely appeared to grieve his loss.

At first, Will and I were terrified that reporters would end up at our door. "This was the reason we came here—to avoid this kind of spotlight," I complained to Will, my tears threatening again. "God, all I seem to do is cry these last few hours."

He wrapped his arms around me, holding me in the deepening shades of two days that had seemed a weeklong. "You're still in shock, honey. That was a horrible experience yesterday morning. As far as the reporters go, it'll be okay. This town is amazing. They'll protect their principal."

He was right. Only one reporter made it to our front porch, and her knock went unanswered. Will and I ate dinner quietly, watching the birds on the lake, listening to the wind in the trees. Slowly I began to feel the calm facade that I'd carefully developed as my trademark, come back to me, fill me with strength and determination to face whatever had to be done.

"Do you think you should come to the service when they have one? What if the reporters are all still around?"

He concentrated on his food for a moment, then glanced up at me. "I look very different from the way I was then. My hair's largely grey, for one thing. And I'm a helluva lot thinner with a great many more wrinkles." He laughed without mirth, the bitter undertones deeper than even I knew. I put my hand on his.

"I'm sorry. I shouldn't have said that. I'm paranoid. You've been given a pardon, a new name, a new town. You can do whatever you want." I said this last part fiercely, almost defiantly, as if speaking to the reporter whose knocks had echoed through our front hall.

"Em, don't ever apologize for being protective of me. It's perfectly understandable. But we don't have anything to hide, so we'll do this together. I can't say I'm looking forward to being under the scrutiny of the press. It'll bring back too many memories. But, I'm not going to let you do that alone. We have to be prepared for them to ask you lots of questions. We should even be prepared for someone from Ottawa to come and let us know that they know."

I clutched his hand and drank in the spring night air, concentrating on the waves disappearing into the advancing darkness. "We'll cross that bridge..." But I didn't believe, wouldn't believe, that this might be the end of the sanctuary that had been so perfect for the last two years. Burchill was our home.

On Sunday morning, the only venture outdoors was Will's trip to the local Tim Horton's for coffee and bagels. We both planned to huddle in our home. No one from Ottawa summoned. Edgar, in a brief early morning telephone call, let me know that school could begin on Monday as usual.

After breakfast, I sat in my study, looking out at the trees rocking softly in the wind, writing my speech for the assembly I'd decided to hold the next morning. I'd asked Reverend Whitmarsh to conduct a short memorial ceremony to give the children an opportunity to mourn Nat and to help them deal with the intrusion of death into their young minds and hearts. The 'Grief Support Team' from the school board was scheduled to spend a couple of days with us, counselling those who needed it.

Will, from his studio in the side yard, saw him first. I, my view obscured by the trees, only heard the footsteps on the front porch. When I jumped to my feet, I saw the top of a grey hat and a tail as the strangers disappeared onto the veranda. The sound of the doorbell caused me to freeze, my heart pounding.

CHAPTER 7

When I got to the bottom of the stairs, I heard Will's voice greeting the visitors from the yard, and by the time I reached the foyer, Will had opened the front door. On the porch, hat in hand, stood Walter Ryeburn. Beside him, her eyes huge and expectant, sitting quietly, was a beautiful little collie.

My astonishment abating, I walked quickly toward them and extended my hand. "Mr. Ryeburn, how kind of you to visit. Come in."

Walter Ryeburn ignored my hand in favour of twisting his hat in his hands. "Didn't come to visit, ma'am," he said, his voice deep and rumbling, verging on rudeness. "The missus begged me to bring you Angel here. She wants you to keep her. Nat had so many animals, ma'am. We don't rightly know what to do with them all. Guess we'll have to send most of 'em to some Rescue Society. Annie, she's desperate over Angel. Seems she was Nat's favourite and Annie can't stand the thought of her goin' to the Society. Annie thought you might take her." During his long speech, he hadn't raised his eyes once to look in my direction. The dog, in contrast, kept her sad brown eyes fixed on me, as if begging me to understand.

Past Walter, Will stood quietly. I looked at him and he raised his eyebrows, clearly telling me that it was my decision. "We've never had a dog," I said softly, peering down at Angel's face, her fur soft around her long, aristocratic nose, her tongue pink where she panted as she waited. It seemed to me that Angel knew her life was about to change drastically. "What if we don't know what to do?"

"She's not a pure bred collie. She's got some terrier in her, so she's not as big as most collies. She's been fixed. And Nat trained his animals well. She barks a little at strangers, but that can be a help when you live way out here." He waved his hand as if we lived in the centre of nowhere.

I bent down to Angel and the little dog came right into my arms, gently licked my cheek, all the while her brown eyes never leaving my face. "What do you think, Langford? I think I love her already. How about you?"

"Well, it's a bit of a surprise, but I think I like the idea. Can we do it on a trial basis, Walter? I mean, if we don't get along, we'll give you a call and decide what to do about her then."

"Fine with me. It's the Missus who's so worried, not me. I don't really care." He brought forth a small bag that I hadn't noticed. "Here's some dog food that we had left. She's trained, as I said. Can do tricks and all that. Does her business outside. She's a clean animal. Used to sleeping outside in an animal shelter with all the others."

"Come here, Angel," I said, and the dog pattered into the front hall. Will, still holding the door, turned to let Mr. Ryeburn go toward the steps.

This time Walter Ryeburn turned and looked right at me. His eyes were ice cold, glinting with a hatred that I felt like a physical blow. "Like I said, ma'am, Angel was Nat's favourite." With that, he turned, placed his hat on his head, and walked quickly and stiffly away.

As soon as the door was shut, I said, "That man is so strange, Langford. He looked at me just now as if he could kill me. Yet here he is entrusting Nat's favourite pet to us." I ruffled Angel's fur and rubbed my cheek on the dog's neck. She responded with more kisses.

Will slid down to the floor beside us, his slender hands caressing the dog and me at the same time. "I think you're much better off here, aren't you, girl?" At the sound of his voice, Angel turned and gave a short, soft bark, as if to answer him. We both laughed.

"I think we have a new family member, Will."

"Yup. I think our hearts have been stolen."

The remainder of the day was spent preparing our house for another personality and getting to know one another. I found a big plastic bowl for her food and one for water. Will showed her the lake and talked about getting a leash and a collar. Although we'd never had a dog, we'd had cats in Vancouver, and I realized as the day progressed that we'd missed having a pet. Angel was the easiest, friendliest, sweetest dog I'd ever met, so it was not hard to look back and see how quickly she became beloved.

We discussed where she would sleep and decided that outdoors was just not acceptable. All the while Angel listened, barking her answers softly now and then, gazing at us with trusting brown eyes. If we decided to keep her, we'd bring her to the vet, make sure she'd had her shots, and that she was healthy. And as we talked into the evening, shared our meal with her at our side, the phrase 'if we decide to keep her' entered the conversation less and less.

That night, when we snuggled under our blankets and the cool evening breeze caused the waves to slap the shore noisily but soothingly, Angel herself decided the question of where she would sleep by settling comfortably on the big rug at the foot of our bed. And neither Will nor I objected when, somewhere between the middle of the night and the beginning of day, Angel snuggled between us and distributed plenty of kisses and at least one contented sigh.

The telephone rang, stark and frightening in the silence of the early dawn. I sat bolt upright, heart hammering, and grasped the receiver. Will and Angel watched me carefully.

"Emily, it's Edgar." He rushed on before I could say anything. "It looks like we'll have to keep the school closed today, maybe even for the rest of the week." This time he paused, taking a deep breath. "We've got another murder of sorts."

CHAPTER 8

My fingers involuntarily curled in Angel's hair. The dog looked up, already alert to my emotions, the tension that electrified the hairs on my hand. "What do you mean—a murder of sorts?"

Edgar cleared his throat, tried unsuccessfully to mask his shaking voice. "Someone is clearly insane, Emily. Someone is playing something really sick and dirty." I waited, my breathing shallow and frightened. "Someone killed Nathaniel's pony, Em. And they put it inside the front door of the school, right outside your office."

A chill went through me, stopping my heart for a beat, stiffening my fingers. Angel whimpered and put her head in my lap. Will grabbed my hand and held tight. "Outside my office? How did they get into the school?"

Edgar sounded tired, defeated. "They must've had a key. I never thought about Nat's keys. I never asked. No one else did either. He had keys, of course. And they must have been stolen." He paused. "The forensic team is here and Doc Harrington has examined the corpse. The animal's throat was cut, then it was left to…" Edgar coughed, sounding as if he were choking on the image.

"How did you find out about it, Ed?" My voice was quiet now, a frozen calm washing over me.

"Someone left a message on the tape at the office last night. Coincidentally, I couldn't sleep, so I went into work at five, I figured I could use the quiet time to prepare for the day. The voice is gravelly, can't even tell if it's male or female. Just says we'd better check the school. Mike and I went in. Soon as we saw it, we locked up again and called Ottawa." He sighed, a wounded, confused, angry sound.

"I'll need to get all the records, Ed, so I can start calling parents and the staff. I can ask May to help out."

"You probably need to call Connie and Peter, too. We'll have to do some damage control. Maybe keep this quiet. We could give some other reason for keeping the school closed. Yeah, I guess you better get over to the school, Em. Sorry to have to do this to you."

I hung up and looked over at Will. In the semidarkness, with the beginning of a cloudy day casting a grey light behind him, his eyes looked huge. I told him what happened, my voice strangely quiet and calm. He insisted that he would come with me.

"But I'm more afraid to leave the house unattended and Angel all alone. Whoever did this to Nat's pony…and Mr. Ryeburn said Angel was

Nat's favourite. I know it's not rational, but I'll ask May to come with me." In the end, I did go without Will, but I drove the car rather than walk, and picked up May on the way.

If Will and I were this frightened, I thought, just imagine what parents would be like. They wouldn't want their children to be outside. Edgar was right. We had to keep this quiet for now, but soon they'd need to know the truth. So far, the sickness had been confined to the school and seemed to circle around Nathaniel, but who could know? Forewarned is forearmed, as the saying goes.

May and I were quiet as we headed up the front walk of the school, our shoulders touching, dreading opening that door. Luckily, a heavy rain began to fall. Hopefully, early risers wouldn't see the activity at the school until we were ready for them.

When we reached the front of the school, I was relieved to see Edgar's large frame filling the doorway, blocking our view. "They haven't removed the corpse yet, Emily, May. But it's covered with a sheet. Try not to look. I'll walk you around it quickly and through the other door."

I was not prepared for the odour. The pungent assault on my senses made me think of the animal's suffering and degradation, as it lay helpless while its life poured from its veins. The floor was covered in blood, a deep, rich brownish red that had seeped down the hall and dripped down the stairs toward the gymnasium and staff room.

CHAPTER 9

Edgar walked us quickly past the body to the other end of the office, where a door led into the health room and through to May's office. There was an inner connecting door to my office, where we could enter without stepping into the carnage outside. I immediately went to my private files and got Peter and Connie's home numbers. Using the conference call option, I spoke to the Superintendent and Trustee together.

Following Edgar's advice, I told them not to come to the school, but to get the wheels in motion for closing the school for at least this week and perhaps the entire two that remained of the school year. Both were of the opinion that the public should be informed about the second killing. Connie in particular agreed with me that parents needed to be warned in order to take extra precautions.

It was decided, finally, that a team of office personnel would be assembled within the hour at the board office. Parents would be called, informed about the death of the pony, and told that the school would have to be closed until further notice. They would be cautioned to be very alert, although the case did not appear to be one of aggression against children, but one centered around Nathaniel Ryeburn. If any parents were not reached by telephone, they would be met by the police who were, even as we spoke, surrounding the school building.

The school board Trustees were also to be assembled for a special meeting tomorrow night, to determine whether to keep the school closed only one week, or two weeks early for the summer break, as well as how to best handle the inevitable press coverage. Of course my presence was expected.

When I had finished the call, I stood still in my office, listening to my heartbeat. I looked at May and we threw our arms around each other, holding on for support and strength. I tried to banish the images of Nathaniel and the animal, both oozing their lifeblood along the floors of the school Nat had loved and worked in for so long. The question remained, why? Why would anyone want to kill that gentle, big-hearted man? I closed my eyes and saw him lumbering toward me, smiling shyly, asking me if I wanted him to go out and collect the mail for the day.

"May, why would anyone want to kill Nathaniel? And then underline it by killing an innocent animal? There must be a message in that, but who's it for?"

May sat down heavily and shook her head. "Nat was the sweetest man, almost childlike, don't you think? Plus he was so well liked by everyone, I think because he was such a good listener. You could see people down at the bridge all the time, talking to him."

I sat down too and stared vacantly out the window. I remembered Ruth McEntyer words. "That's something I never knew about Nat. I never... I don't think we really talked about anything other than school." I hesitated. "And his animals. He would tell me lots of stories about them, about this one that was wounded and how he helped it, or about a bird that he found and how he nursed it back into flight. I don't think I ever thought of him separately from the school. Nat and the school building seemed to be, I don't know, almost one. That was pretty callous of me, when I think about it now. As if he didn't exist as a person."

"You're always so hard on yourself. It's amazing how differently you see things! What I saw was that Nathaniel Ryeburn never—and I knew him his whole life—he never talked to anyone the way he talked to you."

I looked up into May's intelligent eyes.

"You're so good, Emily, and you don't even know it. I think it's because your people skills are completely natural to you. You think everyone's the way you are. Nat told you so much about himself, about his life. And you always responded in that perfect way. You always made him feel like you were equals, not the way some principals see a caretaker. He adored you. For everyone else, he was the bridgeman. And that carried a certain stigma in this town or a perceived social responsibility, I guess you might say." May got up and looked out the window, as if picturing Nathaniel by the canal.

"Every day, before coming here, and afterwards, he'd be down by the canal, standing by the locks, oiling them, making sure every gear and gadget was working. And every day you could see people coming up to him and talking, talking, talking. It was a Burchill tradition. All the bridgemen were the town counsellors over the years."

"And Nat, he would just nod and smile and not really say anything. Yet he had this reputation for solving problems, for being quite wise despite his simple demeanour. All the people really did was use him as a sounding board, because he never gave advice, and he never told any of the secrets that were told to him." May laughed. "And that's a rarity in this town, let me tell you. The people just solved their own problems by talking them out. They think they loved and admired Nat, but all they really knew about him was that he was always available, same time, same place every single day. He told you and shared more with you than anyone I've ever seen."

"Thanks for that, May. You always know how to make me feel better. Everything I hear about Nat makes it even harder to believe that anyone would want to kill him. He's just so sweet, always kind and helpful and...and the more I learn about him, the more it just confirms my impression of a gentle giant."

Just then Edgar's face appeared in the doorway. "What's the verdict, Emily?"

I told him that the Board personnel would call parents regarding closing the school for at least this week and perhaps the whole two weeks before the summer break. They had decided to tell the parents the truth about what had happened. A special board meeting would be held tomorrow to make decisions and formulate a plan to handle press releases.

He nodded his approval. "I think closing the school for two weeks is the only way to handle this. I hope that's what they decide to do. The Ottawa people are pretty much already in place around the school, plus some have headed over to the Ryeburns'. No one can figure out what the hell is going on. How did someone get a horse into the school for God's sake without anyone seeing it? So they're also going to go into the neighbourhood to ask everyone questions. We're going to publish a request in the paper for anyone who saw anything to come forward." Edgar ran his fingers through his hair. His normally calm face was lined with worry and more than that, I saw anger. "We've got to get this bastard who's ripped up our town. Excuse my language, Emily, May."

"It's more than appropriate in these circumstances, believe me." I stood up. "Was there any kind of a message, Ed? Or was the pony supposed to be it?"

"I found nothing, Emily. No written note, no message from the voice on the tape except to get to the school. I guess we're just supposed to figure it out. The press is going to go wild. Nothing like this has happened in the big bad city, let alone a sleepy place like Burchill." He grinned, a lopsided, sarcastic grimace. "Just imagine what a great summer we'll have with the tourists now."

"Is it okay if I search around? Downstairs?" I hadn't known I was going to say it until I'd finished. Edgar and May looked at me, astonished.

"I'll check with Ottawa, but I guess it'd be all right. You got a hunch?"

I glanced at May. "I just have this feeling that Nat would have left me a message. I think he tried to tell me something and I'm missing it. I don't think he'd leave without telling me what happened. I know that's irrational, but I seem to be quite irrational in the last few hours... "

"Once again, more than appropriate in the circumstances." Edgar led us through the door into May's office. "I'll be right back."

May sat at her desk and began to assemble the children's files. "I'll get the family lists and phone numbers ready to fax to the board office and start calling the staff. Emily, are you okay?"

For a moment, I considered. "I think so. At least, I'm calm. I was just thinking about what you said, about how Nat confided in me. If he had some time like Doc said—if he'd been able to think just before he died, in spite of the pain, he would have known that I would likely be the one to find him. Maybe he left me a message. I haven't spent any time thinking about everything and I need to, while the images are still right before my eyes. I think I need to look over the death scene. Maybe something will come to me. In the meantime, I'll help you wake the staff a little earlier than usual and then tell them to go back to sleep."

Later, when May and I were completing the calls to the staff, Edgar came back and told me that Ottawa had finished with the basement and had given their permission for me to go through it. As I descended the steps, the dread came back to me. I wondered what the hell I was doing.

The windowless room was cool and dry, like a wine or fruit cellar. The stains from Nathaniel's painful death darkened the floor and looked grotesque in the fluorescent lighting. I stood in the middle of the room, listening to the humidifier sighing inside the furnace.

I imagined Nathaniel, remembered his talking to me down here on several occasions as we surveyed the supplies, filled out maintenance requests or purchase orders. *"Mrs. Emily..."* He would never quite call me Emily, despite my requests to do so. *"Looks like we need to order some paper towels. Have ya thought about puttin' in them hand blowers? Sure would save a pile o' money down the road."*

I turned to look inside the electrical room. Here I found the remainder of his pictures, all pinned carefully to the bulletin board amid health and safety notices and warnings. In one, Angel looked up at the camera, her soft brown eyes wide. I could only think she looked frightened. Maybe she didn't like the flash of the camera. In another stood the pony, a beautiful brown and white, sleek animal. How could anyone have left it to die that way? Several photos were of cats, some birds, rabbits, and one of Nathaniel's parents, obviously taken a long time ago, for they both stood ramrod straight, faces unwrinkled by time.

They were several inches apart, not touching, unsmiling, and that frozen image told a story of cold, unspoken aggression and even hatred. Imagine growing up in that high-ceilinged, dark house with these unloving, icy parents. Was Nat ever hugged or kissed as a child? Had he found comfort in the solitary, repetitive activities of the bridge? Or in the companionship of animals that had been abused and discarded? Why had he left home all those years ago, and more importantly, why return after his escape?

I plucked one of the pictures from under its pin. Nathaniel was in the background, showing off the sheen of the little pony, the dogs and cats around his feet, and a ribbon of some sort that one of the animals had obviously won. I studied his big, flat face, his pockmarked skin, his unruly and always greasy hair, his wide, guileless eyes. I had shamefully been struck by Nathaniel's unattractive exterior when first I met him, but soon I'd forgotten that in the light of his peaceful, industrious, kind and giving nature. Now in the stark fingers of light that hit this old photograph, I could see the ill-formed features and misshapen nose that combined to make Nathaniel Ryeburn unappealing, even ugly, if one judged by looks alone.

"You know, Mrs. Emily, birds are actually very smart. Especially crows. After that crow's wing healed, he hung around people like he was one of us. I had to capture him again and take him way out to the reserve so he'd get used to the woods again. He looked at me with such hurt eyes when I told him to fly away. He turned his head sideways and listened to me talkin'. He knew what I said. He just didn't want to believe that I didn't want him around. But he was gettin' too close to the kids in the park and all the parents was complaining. I figured sooner or later someone'd shoot him. I hope he's happy out in them woods."

I, distracted, busy, thinking, would give some inane reply, such as "I'm sure he is." Then I'd ask, "Nat, what about salt? Do we have enough for the driveway for winter?"

"Look here, Mrs. Emily. I never showed this to nobody else. You won't tell, will you?"

Of course, Nat. I'll never tell anyone. I promise. Would I even remember this exchange? It seemed so inconsequential at the time.

"There's a secret little box right here. Don't know what the guy who built this place was thinkin'. Like you said, maybe it was one of them bomb shelters, and this little cupboard was for hidin' valuables. Look."

And one of the grey concrete bricks, which looked exactly like all the others, swung open at his touch to reveal a safe-size compartment tucked inside the wall. *"I jes' keep some personal papers and special pictures in there, Mrs. Emily. Hope you don' mind. Ain't got much of a private place at home, doncha know."*

That's really interesting, Nat. Of course I don't mind. Lynda's complaining that her trash didn't get emptied last night. Are those part-time cleaners listening to you?

Had I really been that careless with him, or did the syndrome that May had been talking about cloud these memories? Am I too critical of myself?

Was the picture clutched in Nat's hand a signal to go and look inside his little hiding place? Or was it something else entirely? Or perhaps simply the last gasp of a man trying to hold onto his life, and the parents and animals he loved so dearly.

I went to the wall next to the electrical room, my fingers skimming over the brick surface, looking for something that would tell me where the safe was. After a few minutes, I found it. The mortar around one of the bricks wasn't actually mortar. It was a steel surface that, when pressed, acted as a spring that caused the 'brick' to swing open.

"I never showed this to nobody. You won't tell, will you?"

Inside, I could see some loose papers, a handful of pictures, and a small brown book. The papers proved to be pay stubs, holiday time sheets, seniority notices and so on. The pictures were more of the same—dogs, cats, ponies, birds. I reached in and drew the book out. It was an old leather diary with a snap that was locked.

"If anythin' ever happens, Mrs. Emily, would you get rid of this here stuff for me? Wouldn't want nobody readin' my personal stuff, doncha know?"

I understand. I promise. Now, what about those loose tiles in..?

I closed the safe and went back to the electrical room. Several keys hung neatly on hooks, mostly labelled. One hook held a few unlabeled, smaller keys. I tried each of them in the diary lock. The last one, a small gold key, opened it immediately. Inside, I glimpsed the tiny, cramped scrawl that resembled Nat's writing. I locked it again.

Although I could never later explain why, even to myself, I placed the diary and the key in my pocket. There was no conscious thought of hiding anything from Edgar, or the law. It was only a desire to keep Nat's secrets, whatever they were, safe. He'd given his trust to me, and I was bound by a promise. I was convinced there could be nothing significant in Nat's scribblings. Or so I told myself later.

CHAPTER 10

At the time, I simply went to the electrical room and began to remove the pictures without much thought at all. Flattening them out, I studied each one more carefully. To my biased eye, one influenced by the murders, I thought I could see terror and hatred in every animal's look. A current of fear shot through my spine and I swung around, staring into the empty basement. Shaking myself, I took the pictures and hurried up the stairs.

Edgar and Constable Ducek stood at the end of the hallway.

"I brought Nat's pictures up with me. I hope that's okay. I thought his parents should have them." The diary weighed heavily in my pocket, but I ignored it. I knew I sounded breathless, wondered if I sounded guilty. But Ducek only nodded absently.

"Good idea," Edgar said, patting me on the shoulder with uncharacteristic affection. "No clues have been found, Emily. Ottawa is stumped and so are we. Haven't even been able to get anyone in the neighbourhood to say they saw a pony, or even a truck that could've carried a pony. So either they arrived in the middle of the night or so early in the morning no one happened to be up."

"They?"

"Or he, she, I don't know. Seems likely the pony was given some kind of drug to make it pass out and lie down, or else it was well trained. Did Nat train the animals as well as care for them?"

"His father mentioned that he trained his animals well. And Langford and I have taken in one of his dogs and I must say, she's amazing." *Those animals are really smart, Mrs. Emily...*

"Interesting. So it could be that we have a very well trained, compliant animal that would have been easily and quietly led up the street and through the front door. Or else was obediently loaded into and unloaded from a truck. We'll know more about the potential use of drugs when the autopsy's finished on the horse," Constable Ducek said. "I hear the school's to be evacuated for the week at least, and maybe for the summer. That's probably a good idea, I guess."

"You sound doubtful, Constable Ducek," I prompted.

"It's just that it may make it very difficult to come back here. The summer might actually blow everything out of proportion rather than allow the fear to abate. Plus it may be exactly what our murderer wants."

"Surely it wasn't done in order to evacuate the school."

Ducek shrugged his big shoulders. "Anything is possible, believe me. I have the feeling the pony was a message. Maybe the killer was looking for something and didn't find it. Maybe the pony was killed the way it was and placed where it was in order to deter re-entry for a while. The culprit would have to know that in a small town like this one, pressure would be put on to evacuate, despite a loss of two weeks of school."

"But wouldn't that just draw attention rather than the opposite? Wouldn't the culprit know that the school is going to be watched?"

"We won't have the personnel to give it round the clock supervision though, believe me. Once again, the culprit must be familiar with small town budgets and politics. If a couple of days go by and nothing happens, you can bet the night watch is going to be drive-bys only, probably left up to your little staff, Edgar."

"This might be the one time I hope the press makes a big deal out of everything," Edgar said.

We were silent for a moment, each of us contemplating the situation. Then as if by agreement, we moved apart, I toward my office, Edgar down the hall, and Ducek to speak to his partner. I arrived at the office just as the pony's body was being loaded into a large black truck at the front door. May came out and followed my gaze as the Ottawa officers and coroners struggled with the ropes and pulleys that held the large carcass.

"Everything's in place, Emily," May said gently. "The school board officials are calling all the parents. I don't imagine too many of them will be upset by the closing. They'll be scared to death to let the kids out at all, let alone come to the school. They'll probably wonder about report cards, though, just in case we stay closed the whole two weeks."

I felt dazed, distracted, and had to pull myself back into the conversation with May. Often she amazed me. Her thinking was so clear and she was able to pick up on details that overwhelmed me. "You're right, May, I will have to do something about the report cards. Particularly if we end up being closed early for the whole summer. The staff will have to be allowed to come in and complete all the records, sign the reports, get the..."

I mumbled to myself, walking into my office, and put the wheels in motion. Once I had the telephone in my hands, I began to feel in charge again. Arrangements were made for staff to come into the school and get their computers and any records they needed to work at home on report cards. Ed, obviously feeling embarrassed, had to accompany them to their classrooms.

The rest of the morning sped past. It was well past one o'clock when May's small dark face peered around at me. "I'm starving, Em. I'll buy you lunch at the Inn."

Realizing I was starving, too, I smiled up at her from my laptop and sighed. "May, that's a marvellous idea. Except we'll let the school board pay for it. Dealing with a situation like this is absolutely above and beyond the call of anyone's duty."

After talking to Will, gathering up my papers and computer, and stuffing everything in the car, I drove us to the Burchill Inn. The day that had begun cloudy and grey had turned into a solid stormy one. The rain was falling straight down, puddling in the dry grass, soaking the budding flowers, giving no sign of letting up. June was still off-season for tourists in Burchill, but the townspeople had obviously decided to spend their rainy lunch hour at the Inn, for the dining room was almost full. May and I sat down at an empty table for two, just below a Langford Taylor painting, a little wet, a lot tired. I sighed and looked around, appreciating, even more deeply than usual, the ambiance of this room.

The colors were pastel, mostly mauve and pink, with lace tablecloths and dark blue napkins. The furniture was fashioned after the 1860's. Some of the pieces were even dated from that time. Paintings and knickknacks graced the walls and mantels (of which there were three), all native or local artistry. One of my husband's best oils had a prominent place above a marble mantelpiece. All of the fireplaces were electric, but in the winter, the glow of the 'fake' fires was still romantic and cozy. The soft lighting was welcoming and comforting after the horror of the pony's death and the relentlessness of the pouring rain.

"Bill and Marjory have done a great job with this place, haven't they?" May sighed as I nodded in agreement.

We said hello to the many people we recognized and they all gave us their sympathy at our loss of Nathaniel. Kindness prevented them from asking questions and once again I appreciated the true friendship of a small town. Diane West, our resource teacher, and an author of note in the community, was sheepishly taking advantage of a free afternoon to meet with her agent. Teddy Lavalle, the much-loved chef of the Inn, was out front talking and laughing with his customers. Michael Lewis, artist/police volunteer, smiled sympathetically at us. Dr. Ron Harrington, the town vet who seemed to love animals far more than humans, appeared haggard and gave only a feeble greeting.

Most of the other tables were filled with familiar faces such as Peter and Ellie Smallwood, Nick and Mary Jo Samuels. They all glanced at May and me often, but their looks were supportive and empathetic, I thought, and not once did they approach our table with a query.

Only Nick Samuels came over and stood by the table. He talked quietly and, I thought, with true concern.

I had forgotten about Nat's diary until I sat down, feeling it bulge against my thigh, my skirt flaring out unnaturally. Feeling a flash of guilt and an electric spark of excitement at the same time, I patted it down while my leg slid under the tablecloth.

We were still speaking with Nick when Bill Percival appeared in the doorway to the kitchen. His round red face lit up with delight. "Ladies! I'm so glad you came over. You deserve a break from all that stress and trouble!" Bill was a loud, flamboyant man who seemed to want to be the stereotype of an Inn Keeper, as if he were the 'master of the house' from *Les Miserables*.

"Where's Marj?"

"Oh, she's here, May, but off in the kitchen supervising as usual. Leaving Teddy to do his usual schmoozing! So I'm all alone in here, serving these brave souls who have come our way. I just might have to call Ruth to throw on her uniform and come on over if this keeps up. How about something to warm your insides, like your favourite martini?" Bill literally said this with a flourish, almost bowing to May, his clipped British accent even more pronounced than usual.

I almost giggled, a reaction of stress and fatigue. "Not for me, Bill. I want a glass of merlot. That'll warm me just fine, thanks."

"Martini for one, then, and a glass of the lovely merlot." He disappeared behind the bar.

May looked right at me and crossed her eyes. Once again I was afraid of erupting into huge inappropriate laughter. Everyone in town would soon think I was on the verge of a nervous breakdown. "Tell her to stop, Nick," I begged. "I'm too tired and stressed to resist guffawing in public."

"Huh! A loud guffaw would do this place good! It's getting a little uppity in here," Nick returned, laughing.

"And don't let me have more than one glass of wine," I added. "I have to drive."

"We could always call Alain to pick us up. He's practically next door. After what we've just been through, I'm not promising to stick to only one martini." May's dark eyes roamed the restaurant, stopping to gaze at *Lost Ring Island*, Will's painting. "I still think that's such a great story, how you lost your ring on that island and years later Langford paints it for you."

"You're such a romantic, May." I could feel myself blushing, cursed my fair skin for still betraying me, despite the other defence mechanisms I have been able to perfect. I never could lie, and I felt uncomfortable that May believed the story I'd told her about *Lost Ring Island*. If she knew the truth...Bill's noisy return to the table interrupted my thoughts.

"Here we are, ladies." He placed May's martini in front of her, swept a wine glass onto my place, showed me the wine bottle, and proceeded to pop the cork. He continued to speak as he went through each of these motions. "You must be exhausted and in such a state! I'm so flattered that you picked my little restaurant to rejuvenate in. Poor Nathaniel! He was such a sweet man. I can't believe someone would want to kill him. Why, Friday this place was filled with reporters. Didn't take them long to clear out yesterday, though. Guess someone more important was killed somewhere else. Poor Nat. Now I guess no one is paying attention. I heard from a few customers earlier that the school is being kept closed though." The last was said not quite as a question, but close enough.

"No one's told you then, Bill." I took a deep breath, surprised that I had to steady my voice before speaking. I was astonished that no one else had told him, particularly Ruth McEntyer, who often worked here part time. Obviously she was too busy calling the neighbours and she hadn't gotten around to talking to Bill yet. Perhaps there still weren't too many, outside of parents of the school children, who'd been informed about what had happened. "Someone killed Nat's pony and left it at my office door, inside the school. Some kind of message they think."

Bill froze, the wine bottle still clutched in his hand. His eyes were wide and his face paled. He looked genuinely shocked. "Message? What kind of...?"

"No one has any idea."

"Someone is pretty sick, I'd say," Nick said, his voice filled with disgust.

Bill blinked, then poured a little of the wine in my glass to taste.

When I nodded my approval, he filled the goblet to the rim. "Bill, enough. You don't want me to be tipsy on a Monday afternoon, do you?" I looked up at him, smiling, and saw that his eyes were still wide with shock. It seemed ironic that it appeared he was taking the death of an animal somewhat harder than the death of a human being.

He shook his head. "Sorry, Emily, but I just can't...I guess that means the reporters will be back and our little town made a circus again."

I had my own private fears along those lines, but I was surprised to hear that Bill did. "It might mean a full house again, Bill."

His smile was thin and forced. "I'd rather have no one than..." He carefully wiped the wine bottle of its slow moving red drops, concentrating on that small act rather than meeting our eyes. He sighed. "Let me tell you our specials to get our minds off all this tragedy." And he recited, with something close to passion, the tempting list of dishes that Theodore Lavalle had created for the day.

Once May and I had chosen—she a creamy pasta dish with shrimp and crab and I a small pepper steak with roasted vegetables—Bill went away and left us sipping our drinks and nibbling on bread. Nick returned to the table right next to us. I tried very hard to ignore the fact that he appeared to be listening over my shoulder.

Within a couple of minutes, though, we were engrossed in conversation and I forgot everyone else in the room. May and I never have trouble talking, and this day, despite its horrors and its shocks, was no different. We were discussing the latest special education cutbacks and didn't notice Marjory Percival enter the room.

"Hi Emily, hi May," she said, standing close to our table and speaking in a loud, unnatural voice. I literally jumped.

"Oh, hi, Marj," May said calmly, as I swallowed my wine and tried not to look as though my nerves were still shattered.

"Marj, I didn't see you. How are you?" As I turned to her, I was struck by the paleness of her face, the largeness of her pupils, the way her lips twitched from a smile to a frown and back again.

Marjory was much younger than her husband, though he hid his age very well. At this moment, she looked as though the age difference were reversed. She was a thin, petite blond with wide blue eyes, whose classic features were normally extremely attractive. Coupled with her British royalty accent, Marjory Percival was a woman who turned heads.

"I'm okay. How are you ladies doing out here? How about some water?" She went to the sideboard and filled our glasses with water and lemon.

"Is this yours, Emily?" To my embarrassment, May held Nathaniel

Ryeburn's diary in her hand.

"Yes, yes, it's—it's mine—from school..." Aware that I sounded odd, I took the little book and stuffed it into my purse. "It must have fallen out of my pocket..."

I could feel everyone's eyes on me. I felt their questioning looks at the loud, unnatural sound in my voice. Every movement in the room stopped momentarily. It seemed to me that everyone was looking at me, gazing pointedly at the stolen diary. I was uncomfortably aware of Nick's stare from the table next to us. Marj appeared not to notice and left to fill other patrons' glasses with water. May, her eyes filled with curiosity, blessedly said nothing.

I shook my head. My old paranoia was resurfacing. It was hard not to be shaken by the events of the last few days, though, I told myself forgivingly.

We indulged ourselves that afternoon with lots of wine and martinis, fresh warm multigrain bread *with* butter, our meals, and a shared Apple Betty with ice cream and coffee at the end. Bill and Marjory were attentive, witty and yet not intrusive. May and I talked a lot about Nat, and in our own way, gave tribute to his life and work.

The dining room slowly emptied until we were the only customers remaining. Alain Reneaux did drive us both home, after all, some time after six o'clock, after the Burchill Inn had paid the bill for one of the longest lunches in history.

It was still pelting rain when I let myself into the house, noticing the light in the workshop out in the yard. The front hall was lit up and I could smell the fragrance of logs in the living room fireplace. As soon as the door opened, Angel appeared at my feet. Giving a small cry, she lay down, paws spread out, begging for hugs. Which she got, plenty of them, me down on the floor, snuggling and petting and putting my face in her fur. After a few minutes I shook out my coat, took off my wet shoes, and went upstairs to change into a robe.

There was a note on my pillow. "Almost done! If the fire goes out, I brought in more logs to light it up again. Love ya, Will." Which was how I ended up in the chair by the fire, feet propped up, dog snuggled in beside me, coffee in hand, reading Nathaniel Ryeburn's diary.

At first I felt guilty, prying, but as I got used to the scratchy writing, I was drawn into a story so well written, so intriguing, so terrifying, that I might have been reading fiction written by a great author. In fact, had events not happened the way they did, I might never have believed a word of it.

CHAPTER 11

The Life of N. Ryeburn by N. Ryeburn
The struggle always begins at dawn. I lie on my back, staring at the ceiling, tracing the tiles with tired eyes. Prayers and petitions, promises to Our Mother, fill my soul with strength. I vow never to let it happen again. I get up, pour myself a small glass of milk, and go into the bathroom. I see my face in the mirror—large, shadowed, my eyes dark with sleep and horror—and I hardly believe it is really me. In my mind, I am still a young boy, eyes unclouded, face unobscured by hair, lines, time, by cruelty and weakness. I force myself to shower, to shave, to prepare my body for a day with people. My heart pounds at the thought of seeing them. Their faces are expectant, their lives unfurled before me, wanting me to relate. Except for her, they do not really see ME.

I sat up straight, my own heart pounding. This writing looked like Nathaniel's small, compact and scratchy style. But the words were so unlike his simple, childlike speech. The language did not match the Nathaniel Ryeburn I thought I knew, or at least had a working relationship with. "*I never showed this to nobody else. You won't tell, will you?*"

In this journal, no hint of the shy, country 'accent', the misuse of grammar, the slight deferential way of speaking. "*I jes' keep some personal papers in there, Mrs. Emily. Hope you don' mind. Ain't got much of a private place at home. Wouldn't want nobody readin' my personal stuff, doncha know?*"

And who was the 'her' to whom he referred? A secret love, his mother? I felt that I was, prying, laying open what appeared to be some kind of confession or treatise of a life lived in sadness and regret. Yet I kept reading, fascinated, frightened, intruding yet compelled to continue.

Burchill is asleep every morning when I open the door of my father's house and step onto the dock. In summer, there is an orange tinge over the horizon, but in winter it is deathly quiet and relentlessly dark. In those times, my eyes must adjust to the blackness. I must shuffle along the dockside listening to the sounds, acquainting myself with the environment before I can proceed. The front porch is only a few steps from the canal, and even in the winter, I can hear the water lapping against the sides of the locks. A faint fishy smell has permeated the walls of my ancestral home. I can smell it in the living room. It invades every pore of my body from here onto the canal walkway.

In the quiet, I can hear the past echoes of fishing boats and pleasure crafts and their loud, crude owners who shout impatiently at me or at each other. In the silence, I can still hear the voices.

I am the bridgeman, as my father was before me, and as his father had been before him, down the ages of my family history like a brand. And yet now it is a lost art, no longer respected, no longer needed, in the age of computers and electronics. I am the son who will see the end of my family's profession, the end of Ryeburn history, the completion of lives lived in serving others for whom the service went unnoticed or unappreciated. I am the last true bridgeman. I deserve no more than this ignoble end.

Tears sprung into my eyes at the power of these words. I thought of Nathaniel Ryeburn's strong, yet unassuming, presence as he gave one of his infrequent smiles, usually apparent only when he talked about his animals and his dreams.

"Some day I hope to have a farm, Mrs. Emily. Mebbe when I retire and my parents...when I kin sell the house, I kin buy a nice farm in the country an' take all my animals with me an' get me some more an' live quiet-like." His big head was nodding, the rare smile lighting his face into something almost attractive, appealing in its openness and the raw hope that it displayed. "*Yeah, I'd sure like that.*"

Yet if this chronicle before me was truly written by this same man, his life had been lived in hopelessness. He saw himself in the darkest of lights, never knowing that the people who 'didn't see him' would mourn his death as if it were the passing of a hero, not the end of the history of an undeserving nobody.

It is in the summer when my work on the dock is full. It is in the summer when the voices are loudest. It is in the summer when the people come.

Each day, with the sun barely peering over the horizon, I stand at the canal edge, hands on hips, sniffing the air. I can tell how many boats will come through just by the weather. It is the rich who mostly use the locks now, the ones with the loud yachts and huge cavernous monstrosities that are practically ships, and which the men use as measures of their masculinity. The women use their words, spitting obscenities at me or the youngsters who work for me, screaming at us if they are not allowed to go first or even second into the locks, hurling vindictive at the slowness of the process, as if we have control over how fast water flows. I am constantly surprised and frightened by their passion, wondering if they know how their anger twists their faces into an ugliness that almost matches my own.

When the rare woman passes by with a smile, a nod and a thank-you, I cannot help but be caught in her beauty, in the light of her smile, in the absolute astonishment of kindness and the loudness of a sweet gentleness that feels like feathers and silk and fur. That is when I dare not look up, lest she see the glare of my need, the nakedness of my weak and sickly soul. The stain of my deeds, the flush of my anger as I turn its full force onto the animals, hating them for their compliance as much as I despise myself for mine, might leak from my space into this woman's, and her kindness will turn to horror and disgust. For within my eyes she might glimpse the maggot that lives underneath.

Just as I never look at HER, afraid she will discover the person who really inhabits this hideous body. The outward repulsiveness is only a small reflection of the ugliness that writhes beneath. I long to turn my eyes on her face, feast on her smile and the melody of her voice as she asks me my opinion—my OPINION! Or how I am feeling—HOW I AM FEELING—and oh God, oh Mother Mary of God, I wish I were not the monster that I am, fervently wish I could return the look she has given me, touch the hand that rests so innocently and friendly upon my sleeve. But I dare not, for she, with her insight and intelligence and connection to people, would instantly see me for what I really am.

So I shuffle beside or behind her, eyes down, voice disguised, hungers abated, evil a thick pounding in my head. A voice in the background, noise as grating as the sound of people's voices on the canal, the monster never leaves me, even as I stand beside her, humbled and awed by her exquisite acts of friendship and affection. Even surrounded by the light of her goodness, the horror that lives within me will, as long as my heart continues to beat, be reawakened by the dark of night—each and every night—no matter the prayers and petitions and promises and memory of her smile. It will not ever leave me. I deserve no more smiles, no more friendship, no pity, no love, no feather or silk or fur, no soft skin touching my hand in affection or even respect.

I stopped, a knot of tension in my neck and a nausea spreading from my stomach to my throat. Was this really written by Nathaniel? From my limited experience with his writing, it looked like his. Yet this language, this relentless self recrimination, the obsession and violence contained in the words, did not in any way reflect the man who came to work at the school day after day or who stood by the locks nodding and listening to the people who passed by to talk to him.

Who was the woman reflected in these pages, the one to whom he gave the attributes of 'insight and intelligence and connection to people'?

How could she have missed his self-hatred, never discovered his hidden violent nature, never saw behind his mask? How much 'light of goodness' could the object of affection in this story have had if she did not ever notice his deep and unabated sorrow? And why had I, who had worked with him day after day, never known or seen or even suspected what lay beneath his gentleness?

I looked up into the orange and red flames in my fireplace and my hands absently stroked the sleeping dog's silky fur. Was this diary a work of fiction? Was it Nathaniel's sick joke on me, to whom he practically bequeathed the tome? Had he hoped I'd read it while he was still alive? Was he watching for some kind of change in my attitude toward him, as evidence I knew the truth? Was he exacting some kind of revenge on the rest of the village by pretending to be someone he was not and then laying it all out in writing? Was he laughing at all of us? What was the horror that lived within him?

I pictured the Nathaniel I had met day after day, the one with the big, gentle hands, the shy sideways glances, the soft voice that seemed odd emanating from such a large man. I remembered how kind and sweet he was with the children, how accommodating and helpful with the teachers, with me. Astonished by how completely I had been fooled, I kept reading, hungry for some kind of explanation.

All of Burchill sets their clocks by me, as they did with my father before me. At precisely 5:30 every morning, I am up checking the huge joints of the swing bridge, even in winter, sometimes oiling, sometimes cleaning, sometimes chipping ice. One by one, as the lights snap on and the people begin to enter the day, they start out at different times to go to work. So many pass the canal, so many stop to talk. Their voices go on and on, like the water flowing through the locks, like nails on a chalkboard.

Yet I stand there, morning after morning, letting them flog me with their grating sounds, their faces open to the new day, their minds elsewhere, already at work, or back home with a problem, worrying or whining or complaining or judging or damning. Little do they know whom it is they stand beside. If I could only tell them, they would be reassured that their lives are harmless, that they need not worry, that their sins are nothing. I could forgive them, send them more happily on their way, but I do not. I cannot.

I stand looking down, nodding, praying they will not touch me, ashamed that they do not see me. I never gossip. I never utter an unkind word. I do not tell their secrets, yet I know them. They pour their hearts out to me, confessing, seeking resolution. I never give advice. I never answer. I nod. I give them space. I allow them to speak to whatever gods they need to get in touch with. And the irony is never lost on me. It is my penance.

At that moment, lightning flashed in the windows, followed by a roll of thunder, and the lights went out. Except for the dying embers of the fire, the living room was plunged into utter darkness. The rain kept pelting against the windows, and other than a sigh from Angel, a crackle from the fire, a deep silence followed that first burst of anger from the sky.

The diary was bathed in too little light, the scrawl indecipherable. I sat listening to my heart pound, jumped when the next crash filled the heavens, started when the lightning threw the living room into daylight once again. Still Angel sat warm and trusting beside me. Still I sat, unable to move or think.

When the door opened, Angel lifted her head and so did I as Will entered, covered by a huge black umbrella and carrying a flashlight. He unfolded the umbrella, shook it out and stood it against the wall, closing the front door quickly. Then he turned on the flashlight, pointed it down at his knees, and started toward the living room. Before either of us could utter a word, Angel jumped from the chair, raced to the window and buried herself behind the curtains, growling and crying, uttering the most heart wrenching sounds I had ever heard from any animal.

CHAPTER 12

"Will, what's the matter with her?"

"Where are you, honey? I can't see."

"Here, in the chair by the fire." At last I roused myself, and in the semidarkness, I reached out for Will's cold wet fingers. "Angel, it's Will. It's just Will. Come here, girl." The growling and whimpering continued, bringing tears to my eyes.

"Maybe she's afraid of storms."

"But she sat right here, right beside me, she didn't move when the thunder and lightning came both times. Angel, Angel," I coaxed, my voice soft.

Suddenly the room was full of light again as thunder shook overhead and lightning illuminated the spot where Angel stood, her trembling visible behind the curtain. Her whimpering was terrible to hear, a sad, frightened, lonely sound.

I made my way slowly in the once-again-darkened room and got down on my hands and knees beside her. Quietly and smoothly I pulled the curtain back. She made no protest as I wrapped my arms around her shaking body and gently put her on my lap. We sat there for a long time, that little dog and I, our hearts pounding together, not moving, even though the thunder and lightning intruded one more time. I whispered in her ear, not because I thought she could understand, but because I wanted her to hear in my voice the comfort and love and reassurance I wanted to give her. Slowly the trembling stopped and her whimpers ceased, and she relaxed in my arms.

Will crawled up to us, put his arms around both of us, and we stayed that way through the next round of storm lashings, until the thunder and lightning seemed to be moving away from the lake and the top of our house. The rain still poured relentlessly on the roof and down the windows. Just then, the lights snapped back on.

I placed Angel gently on the floor and Will helped me to my feet. He pulled the curtains back and patted the dog, still standing rooted to the spot, talking quietly to her. "Did I scare you when I came in the door in the dark with that big umbrella, girl?"

Angel looked up at him and her tail began to wag. "Don't be scared any more, little one, it's okay. Mommy and Daddy are here."

Despite the decidedly unfunny last few hours, I began to laugh. "Mommy and Daddy? Why, darling, I think you are completely smitten!"

"Hey, look who's talking." Will pulled me to him and we stood there in the window, holding each other, as Angel tapped her tail on the hardwood floor. "Does anybody want dinner, or are you still too full from lunch?" Angel's tail tapped louder and she gave one of her trademark soft barks in answer.

"Looks like someone will join you, but I don't think it'll be me," I said. "I'll be there in a minute. Maybe I'll have a bowl of soup or something."

Will and Angel headed for the kitchen, while I closed the diary, placed it on the end table, and picked up the flashlight from the floor. Will was filling Angel's dish when I walked in, ready to place the flashlight on the counter. The moment I entered, she looked straight at me as if she had never seen me before, and bolted from the kitchen. Once again, we could hear the whimpering and growling. Shocked, both Will and I stared at the object in my hand as if it were a gun. And indeed, we came to the conclusion at exactly the same time that that's exactly what it was to Angel—a lethal weapon.

Suddenly the words I had just read in Nathaniel Ryeburn's diary leapt back into my head: *I deserve no more smiles, no more friendship, no pity, no love, no feather or silk or fur, no soft skin touching my hand in affection or even respect. The stain of my deeds, the flush of my anger as I turn its full force onto the animals.* Feather, silk, or fur. The flush of anger turned into violence on the animals. Had he beaten this poor dog with a flashlight or other similar weapon? I could scarcely believe what I was thinking, yet I had obviously not known Nathaniel Ryeburn at all.

Without a word, Will buried the flashlight at the back of a drawer and pulled out some of our candles. "Guess this is what we'll use if the lights go out again."

It took us longer this time to calm Angel and to coax her back into the kitchen for food. Once she had nosed around long enough to convince her that the weapon was no longer in sight, she began to relax. Soon she had eaten and was sitting at Will's feet as he ate his dinner. I sat across from him, nursing another cup of coffee, wondering if I would be able to sleep with all this caffeine and the lines of the diary humming in my head.

As it turned out, I went to bed with Will and Angel, but lay there, face up, long after my husband's breathing was low and rhythmic, long after Angel had curled into a silent ball. I couldn't help myself. Obsessed, I crept out of the bed into the living room, turned on a lamp, folded my legs into my dressing gown, and read.

Each long, painful day is a duplicate of the one before it. One by one, the people of the village come to see me as I work by the canal. They are not attracted by the swing bridge, for they are used to its smooth operation and take it completely for granted. The routine never changes.

Whenever a boat approaches the narrow waters, I spring into action. I change the green light to red, watching as the gates float into place, stopping cars from entering the bridge. Then I set the huge machinery in motion, pulling on the wheel with all my enormous weight to make the bridge swing sideways. After the boat sails gracefully through, I reverse the process, close the bridge, and signal green to any automobiles waiting on the road. Sometimes strangers to the village stand at the canal to watch, but that is not why the residents come to visit me.

Nor are they attracted to my physical appearance. I am almost seven feet tall, burdened with an awkward, blubbery fat that spreads evenly over my body. I always wear the bridgeman's cap, pulled tightly over my curly, still-brown hair. Even by modern, lenient standards, I am very ugly. My flat, bulbous nose covers my face, which is scarred from terrible acne that plagued me in my teens. Nearly hidden by bushy eyebrows, my black eyes are too wide for my flat face and bulge out unnaturally. My mouth is pulpy and unpleasant. Huddled in my striped bridgeman's jacket, I barely peer out at the world, pulling at the visor of my cap with my watery fingers. No one but my animals has ever seen me smile broadly. Occasionally, a twisted grin will curl up at the side of my mouth, giving my face, I think, a less gruesome look. No, it is not my appearance that attracts the villagers.

Yet every day, continuously, someone comes down to the canal to talk to me. Even in the winter, when the cold is biting, someone can be seen standing with me, furiously talking. When only the lake freighters can break through the icy river, I have more time to listen. That is the worst time for me. The wind and cold freeze my nose, my mouth, my soul. Still the voices drone on, shouted above the noise of nature, chirping at me, slicing little pieces of me. Yes, I do know that I am known as wise, as a great advisor, one who can be trusted. People boast that the bridgeman can solve anyone's problems.

If only I could appreciate this reputation as humour, as irony, as the joke that the almighty intended. But all of this praise is heaped on me for one reason only: I never speak. I do not engage in idle talk, although I know everything there is to know about everyone and every occurrence in town. That's because they tell me. Sitting on the edge of the canal, as I go about my business, they pour their hearts out to me. As any psychiatrist knows, people usually solve their own problems by talking about them.

Thus they began to attribute to me the powers of counselling. Yet my only contributions to the conversations are grunts, groans and nods. It is not that I am stupid or disinterested in the people, as many suppose that I am. It is just that I am afraid.

Although no one ever guesses, behind the hat and the eyebrows, my eyes bulge in fear whenever anyone approaches me. I nervously dart to and fro, finding things to do, as the villagers talk. My heart pounds and I sweat heavily, even on winter days. I am terrified of these people, too frightened even to ask them to leave. They take my silence to be acceptance, my nods to be understanding, my lack of confession or complaint on my part to be an ability to handle problems much more adeptly than they.

Over the years my stature in the town has grown until everyone loves and admires the bridgeman. At first, once I became aware of these feelings, I was embarrassed by them. Gradually, my guilt, that terrible gnawing, self-loathing, has increased incrementally with the love and admiration these good people show me. Over the years I have received gifts, letters, even money, proffered with humility, appreciation, even tears.

I am the sole person who knows that they love the man they only think I am. If anyone ever guessed my terrible secret, saw into my dark and perverted heart, I know that they would loathe me even more than I despise myself.

How little I had known about you, Nat, I whispered to the sound of the wind and waves swirling around my house, to the soul that had been this tortured man. Had I noticed your ugliness? Had it meant anything to me that you were big and moved with a kind of grace that was reserved for large, muscular, yet overweight men who had the power and strength to lift and pull and shift things, but whose gait was rambling and awkward, whose body at rest seemed out of place? I saw your face as wide and innocent, Nathaniel, as eager to please, cheerful, dedicated. I saw none of the anger, the violence, the raw wounds that you write about here.

I took a deep, long, slow breath, struggling for reality, wounded by a sense of betrayal, a fear that nothing in Burchill would ever again be what it appeared to be. Yet I of all people knew that masks were worn each day, as Will and I donned ours every morning and walked amid these people as Mr. and Mrs. Taylor, ordinary folk. Who was I to feel betrayed by Nathaniel Ryeburn? His masks—countrified caretaker, beloved bridgeman, devoted son, friend of the people—must have hidden a secret at least as terrible as the one Will and I held. Yet somehow, Nat had allowed his other persona to drag him into an abyss of self-loathing, anger, even violence. Who really was Nathaniel Ryeburn? What was his terrible burden? And what, if anything, did it have to do with his death?

The second reason for the villagers' interest in me is that I am Burchill's Mystery Man. Their fascination with me and with my past probably would have died long ago had I been a talkative or social man. As it is, rumours circulate the town every week and almost always involve me. Strangely enough, it is the people themselves who relate these rumours to me, telling me as if to protect me. Yet I see the hunger on their faces, waiting breathlessly to see if they will be the one person in town to whom I will speak of these things. All of the villagers do know several things about me, because I was born in Burchill.

My parents were quiet, austere people to whom their only son was born late in life. Even as a child, I never took part in ordinary activities. I spent most of my time with my father, helping to work the bridge, or at home with my animals. Children did not like me. I was too quiet, too frightened, too odd. I never knew the language of children. I could never understand their play, their jokes, their antics. I found nothing to say to them. They looked at my ugly face, laughed at me, poked me, even beat me now and then. And though I towered over them from the time I entered school, I could not bring myself to touch their flesh even in self-defence.

When I was seventeen, I disappeared from the village. I was gone ten years. During that time, as far as anyone knew, my parents never heard from me. When I returned, I began to care for my elderly parents and took over the job of bridgeman. It is the ten-year absence that fascinates Burchill. Every week someone offers a new, creative explanation. Anyone bold enough to ask me face-to-face has never received an answer.

What if I were to tell them where I had been? The laughter twists inside me, a sick, live thing. It bubbles to the surface, becoming spittle on my chin. I am nauseous, remembering what happened to that tall, fat, ugly boy in the city. For ten years I allowed myself to abuse and be abused, to reach the depths of degradation, to become addicted to evil and cruelty.

I remember the first time that the depth of my depravity became clear to me, and the shock of my inner self drove me away from the innocence of Burchill.

One day, walking through the field, I stumbled upon the cadaver of what once had been a pure white cat, but which had, in the abuse its body suffered after death, turned slightly grey. There was no forethought in what I did next. I took the body home with me, to my shed, and sharpened my hunting knife. I sliced tenderly through its stomach, opening the flattened, insect-ridden innards to the light, stared at the tiny organs pinched and red inside, stacked so logically and compactly. I quickly found the heart and placed it in my shaking hands, staring at the small dot of bloody tissue that had made this creature live, that had made this animal love that caused a cat to lick and kiss and knead and need.

I knew intellectually of course that it is the brain that does so much of this, that causes these electric impulses called love, yet I could not help but think of the heart as the lifeblood of the brain, and therefore as the source of all feeling.

There was a tremendous rush as I held that little heart in my hand. I sliced and cut and drew out all the parts and pieces that had once been a living, breathing, laughing, jumping, warm creature. What a connection I felt to that deadness! What a thrill went through me as I felt the animal's parts and knew that each one of them was under my control. Apart, in pieces, in layers, cold, reeking with decay, it could not hurt me, yet it was one with me, belonged to me, had no choice but to do my bidding. I was its skin, its movement, its shape, its god, its creator, its destroyer.

And Mother Mary help me, that feeling was a drug to me. I realized it was more powerful than love, more powerful than hatred, more powerful than goodness. It was evil. It was seductive. It became me and I became it.

So for ten years the hunter sought the hunted. Not because they were important to me, but because the act itself was important to me, IS me. Killing, cutting, playing, taking everything apart and putting it back together if I feel like it. Total, complete, control. Transcending them and me and our earthly bodies and joining a dance of destruction.

I hold that little heart in my hand and squeeze.

I was instantly up on my feet, swallowing, breathing, my heart hammering, my vision swimming. I was reading a horror, watching a blood movie, witnessing a terrible accident. This could not be my Nathaniel, the quiet unassuming man who followed me each day, brought me coffee, smiled at me, suffusing his unattractive features in the light of that affection. He could not be a hunter, seeking the kill. He could not hurt a precious animal, not a living, breathing thing. He was kind, gentle, brought birds back to life, nursed puppies to health, tended to creatures even the vet would not touch.

I imagined his big hand in mine, tentatively shaking it the first time we met, and every holiday good-bye after that. I heard his voice, not the voice of this writer, but the voice of Nat, "*Mrs. Emily, you should see that pony's eyes ever' mornin', jes waitin' for his breakfast, whinnying softly in my ear, jes so pritty. I love those animals, ya know? Do ya think I'm soft in the head?*"

"No, Nat, no, it's beautiful how you love them, how gentle you are with them. Everyone admires you for your kindness."

Head down, shuffling away, his shoulders slightly hunched, I believed naively that my words comforted him, made him feel better about himself. I had contributed to his self-esteem. How arrogant of me, how insensitive, how stupid and blind. Who are you, writer? Who were you, Nathaniel? What happened to you? Where did you go? What 'city' do you speak of in which you lost your soul? Were you laughing at us, at me, at everyone who thought you were someone else entirely?

Over the years I have attended church faithfully, sometimes with my mother and father. I dress in my ill-fitting, dark blue suit with blue socks, a white shirt and a blue tie. It is my only other outfit aside from the bridgeman's jacket. At home, I have a red-checkered hunting shirt, which I wear over my jeans. I have small interest in the way of material things and very little feels comfortable on my skin.

On Sundays I squeeze my hugeness into the back pew, fingering my old black Bible. It is a book that my father gave me as a child. Throughout the service, I run my fingers through my curly hair, missing the bridge cap. Whenever anyone looks at me, I stare straight ahead, and those sitting beside me, I am sure, can feel the heat of my nervous sweat. I am always first out the door, never stopping to talk on the front steps as most of the congregation does. My family and I never accept invitations to Sunday dinner, though many people ask.

Until she came along, I had never been seen with a woman other than my mother or those who come to talk to me by the canal. More than that, I had never been caught looking at a woman in a sexual way. The villagers concluded simply that I, in my great wisdom, knew that no girl would likely be interested in me because of my permeating ugliness. So I adjusted, they said, to a life of celibacy, content with hearing confessions on the bridge.

Little do these kind-hearted, self-centered and simple people know that their worship of me, their constant attention to me, plunges me daily into hell.

For I do look at women, and often, with lust and longing in my eyes, if only they took the time to notice. I am especially frightened of my feelings for her.

The 'her' underlined twice, the pen leaving dark lines on the paper, it seemed that this was where Nat lost control—in the presence of someone he obviously admired and perhaps even loved. A small voice in the back of my mind kept saying, "it's you, Emily, Nat was in love with you." Who else asked him for his opinion? Asked him how he felt? Put a friendly hand on his sleeve? Later I was to wish fervently that I had listened to the voice and put the book away, given it to Ed Brennan, anything but keep reading. Yet continue I did, as if I somehow owed it to that other Nathaniel to find out what this Nathaniel had done to him. I still could not believe that 'my' Nat was this perverted, evil person who hated himself so thoroughly, who 'abused and was abused'.

During those ten long years when I was away, I at first traveled everywhere, working at countless different jobs, even in the kitchen of a cruise boat to Europe, searching. Nowhere did I find love or acceptance. Ridiculed, used, degraded, hated, mistrusted, my outer shell proved too thick to penetrate. It was in this time, in each vast city with its impersonal cold, that the desire smouldered and grew and even now begins my struggle each day.

In Burchill, I at least have the bridge. It is my link, my purpose. There is a reason to rise every morning. As the bridgeman, I am needed, relied upon. Inanimate objects have always appealed to me more than people did. Objects do not frighten me. I love that bridge. I enjoy stroking the machinery into action, take pleasure in helping it perform. Beside the bridge, I am small but treasured, needed for myself, not for what I ought to be.

It is ironic that in the years after I returned, I began to attract the villagers' attention. I became aware of their interest slowly, shyly. I never sought their affection and certainly do not want their confidences. Terrified to speak, I would stoically avoid them. Instead of driving them away, my silence acts like a magnet. Now every day, I go through the torture, wishing I could hide away under the bridge forever.

They are good people, though, and this makes my struggles worse. The sins that they confess to me are, in my estimation, as particles of dust in comparison to the mire of my dark soul. Yet I hate them, too, for they use me as all other people have. They have created their own bridgeman, love me for the man they want me to be, and not for who I am. Never do they consider me a person with needs and wants of my own. I am ugly, condemned to a 'priestly' existence through none of my own doing. And the people of Burchill, because they want to, believe that my lifestyle is one of my own choosing. My hatred, my desires, my resentment, well up each day and emerge in the way that I have come to see myself, twisted and ugly. Every morning, after cleansing myself with prayer, I start the day feeling strong and new. By seven, after numerous confessions, problems and confidences from my neighbours, the evil inside me dissipates.

At least to her, I am visible. I am simple, I am kind, I am shy to the point of speaking and smiling little. She can never imagine another side of me. She would never believe that under the overalls of the competent bridgeman is a consummate actor, whose role is worthy of an Oscar. Every day I play my other part, the ill-educated speech patterns, the painful introversion, the asexual touch, the limited vocabulary and thoughts. If only she knew that beneath this cloth lies a man who has participated in evil, abuse, lies, and even murder. If only she knew the tortured ritual through which I go each evening when the bridge has been oiled and coated for the night and I am nearly consumed by the fire within.

If only she knew that my tormentor, my 'partner in crimes' lives among the villagers, too, but unlike myself, accepted as one of the elite. If only she knew that I am the conduit that permitted this evil to leak into the little town of my birth, the innocent enclave unaware of the violence and abuse in its midst.

Again, I stopped, looking up and squinting into the darkness beyond my lamp. I could hear Will's snoring, the waves lapping the shore, the distant hoot of a lonely bird. I shivered in the cool of the storm's aftermath. I wanted desperately to think of this diary as a novel.

What if Nathaniel had enjoyed writing this fiction? What if his hints to me about the diary had been purposely given, hoping I'd read it so he could laugh at me the next time I looked at him with different eyes? Although this explanation still felt like a betrayal, it made more sense than the one these words implied. A partner in crimes? What crimes? In the village? Accepted as one of the 'elite'? In our Burchill? Give me a break, Nat, or whoever you are. Going on seemed easier now. This had to be the work of a sick imagination.

My tormentor found me in Toronto. It's easy to find people like yourself in the alleys and darkness of a big city, under cover of garbage and stench that keeps all others away.

This particular club was in a narrow alley, the back part of a seedy restaurant that fed cheap greasy meals to people who couldn't afford much else. Unless you had been told, you wouldn't know the place existed. The entry looked like the door to a garbage shoot, which in many ways it was. By this time in my life, I had given in to my desires to hurt and abuse, but stopped at killing. In my twisted way, I actually thought I was being good! What a kind, thoughtful human being I was and still am, torturing and injuring and even maiming, but not killing. How generous and restrained!

She would never set foot in a place such as this, nor would I ever wish her to! When I met her, everything she did and said put my life into a different perspective and I have regretted my past and my present more deeply than ever. Most people, as I said, do not know these evil dens exist. But exist they do, even now, in this day of 'enlightenment' and 'civilized' behaviour.

When you enter, you are struck by the aura of degradation, the smell of fear and anger and perversion. It is also the odour of power. The client here becomes the creator or the destroyer. The fate of the heart in your grip is under your complete control. This particular dungeon under the ground is an enormous cave. There is a large stage in the middle of the first cavern as you enter. On either side, long narrow passageways lead off into the darkness. The rooms on either side of these tunnels resemble stables, which, in actual fact, they are. The only privacy is provided by dark red curtains and behind those filthy pieces of cloth you can hear the sounds of cruelty and suffering.

When I entered the Den for the first time, I had some idea of what to expect. I had visited these places in my short wanderings through Europe. Without being aware of it, I had reached the bottom. Here I was, back in my own territory, giving in to my depravities even when I knew I could be caught. I was tired, full of self-hatred and self-pity.

Perhaps I wanted to be discovered. I had entered the den of hell. At this point, had I known, I could have saved myself. I could have made a different decision. But I did not. I had no idea that my action—or inaction—was about to cause a set of circumstances that would involve so many lives.

The show is about to begin, so the strings of lights are dimmed even further, and we all perch expectantly on the folding chairs in front of the stage. There are about twenty of us there, all furtive, staring at the stage, *avoiding anyone's eyes lest they see the need mirrored there. Right now there is not much to look at. The only prop on stage is a gleaming stainless steel table. The curtains part and the women stand there, two of them, tall, thin, emaciated creatures, their faces covered with masks, their bodies oiled and hidden in shadow. For it is not the women we come to see.*

It takes only a few moments for the donkey to be led onto the stage, clopping heavily on the wooden planks, its fur standing straight up on its head and back, quivering in the dampness of the dungeon. For most of us in this room, we of the ugly inclinations, the animal is the part of the show that we have been waiting for.

This time the breath left me and I choked, rising quickly and walking away from the book as if it were alive.

CHAPTER 13

When I got to the washroom, I glimpsed my face, flushed and blotched, in the mirror. I was uncertain as to whether I could keep reading, whether I could ever touch those pages again. I felt nauseous and teary, sad and terrified. Pictures of the Nathaniel Ryeburn I once thought I knew—shy smile, generous, simple, thoughtful, hard working, walking by my side, speaking in low tones, spare but delightful chuckle—kept flashing through my mind. Completely at odds with the vicious, ugly, remorseful yet somehow proud, visions of the writer of this diary.

This Nathaniel Ryeburn held a dark secret for which he was sorry, yet obviously not ready to relinquish. He claimed to be held in its power. Yet wearing that secretive, spying mask was a choice he had made. Had he been peering at me from behind those dark, hooded eyes all this time?

I shivered again, and suddenly, I no longer was able to hold it in. I vomited and sobbed at the same time, letting go of all the horror and filth that had slid down into Burchill and into my life over the last few days.

When I regained a sense of calm, I checked to make sure Will and Angel were still asleep, then fixed myself a cup of hot tea. I stood for a long time in the kitchen, looking out at the sky, watching the lightning flickering over the trees as the storms moved east. Stirred up by the wind, the waves were still fairly rough, splashing against the shore, clawing rocks and sand back with them. Our wind chimes tinkled back and forth, a lonely tune in the stillness left by the thunder and lightning. My hands had stopped shaking. Warmed by the cup, my fingers no longer felt icy.

For a moment, my mind was blank, mesmerized by the movement of the waves back and forth and the leaves swaying with the trees. It was one of those moments when time stands still, when you are aware of the beating of your heart and the breath as it leaves your body, when your life behind you and beside you is a jumble of images and words that have frozen into a mist. I stood for the longest time with my mouth slightly open, as if deeply asleep, unable to fathom what was happening to me or what I should do from here.

When my thought process came back to me, it was a loud, angry voice in my head. I could no longer deny that this diary might have clues to Nathaniel's death. If this writing had actually been penned by Nat, which I still, irrationally perhaps, tended to believe that it could not have been, then his references to his 'tormentor' and the fact that this person lived in Burchill could not be ignored. Yet I was not ready to turn it in just yet. I wasn't sure that I was finished reading.

Despite feeling nauseous and afraid, there was another force that seemed to be propelling me back to those pages, as if obsessed with a horror flick that you watch with one eye, unable to take it in fully yet unable to let it go. Thus I went back to reading. I had to uncover the mystery. I had to know what had led Nathaniel back to Burchill, led him to become someone he was not—and curiosity, disbelief, whatever emotions there were—still remained greater than my fear and disgust.

God help us, we watch and take pleasure in what we see. And when the show is over, we are offered any number of rooms for ourselves. We pay our money and slink off to do whatever hideous deeds in the dark and dankness of the caves.

I turned the page of the diary only to discover a series of lines and drawings, obviously made by the writer, which made no sense to me at all. It seemed as if the author—as if Nat—were letting out his emotions and self-recrimination in some kind of code known only to him. The lines screamed out disgust, fear, anger. The small drawings seemed to curl into themselves, as if he were trying to return to a womb of safety and sanity.

Despite my revulsion at his sexual proclivities, my heart cried out for this Nathaniel, the one tormented and unloved, the one who had succumbed to this power over those poor animals because he could find it nowhere else. When no human being will touch you, when there was no opportunity to become one with another, did it seem so odd that your mind and heart and soul could become twisted and so easily turned to evil? These drawings before me seemed to be a cry for help, a begging of forgiveness. There was something childlike and pathetic about them, as if no words could describe the torture that he went through day after day.

It was almost dawn and the first tentative rays of the sun had pierced through the clouds, orange and pink on the horizon. The birds were ruffling their feathers, calling out softly to make sure everyone was there, beginning the hunt for food.

I heard Angel's paws clipping softly across the floor and I put my arms out for her. She snuggled next to me, head on legs stretched out in front, and sighed contentedly. Had Nathaniel abused her? This sweet, loving, innocent dog? I snuffled my face in her fur, tears edging through again, feeling pity and anger and grief all at once. One hand resting on Angels' silky body, I turned the page of the diary.

He caught me as I came out of the Den that night. Grabbing my arm roughly, he spun me around and held me against the wall of the building. Although I am much taller and larger than he, I couldn't find the strength to fight back. I was spent. My emotions had taken me to the heights of excitement, disgust, fear, and power. I was physically empty, exhausted, extinguished. I could not fight him.

Even in my dazed state, I saw that he had found me and that he saw who I had become, knew all about what I had done, what I was compelled to do. He held the packet in his hand and leafed through them slowly, and even in the darkness I could see them clearly.

"You're going back to Burchill. We have business. Make it soon. Or else." He slipped the package into his jacket and walked away, his footsteps echoing in the quiet night.

I slid to the ground, the dirt and wet of the building seeping through my pants, the harshness of the bricks scratching through my shirt. Tears flowed down my face. A hacking cough of weeping erupted from my lips. I was completely out of control.

His utterance was a command and a threat. I knew what he would do with the package if I did not return, and I simply could not risk it. I could not bear to think that my mother would die knowing her son was a depraved and sickening soul, someone she would never be able to look upon again. Although she had been a cold, unaffectionate mother, she was still mine. And I was tired, needy. He had chosen exactly the right time to appear. How had he known? On reflection after all this time, I believe that it was simply coincidence.

If I had known what was to occur in Burchill, would I have returned upon his command? Would I have chanced that either his threat was empty, or that my mother would never have believed him? Even when he showed her the evidence, would she have turned him away, told herself that the pictures were faked? Of course I will never know, because after that brief, quickly uttered command in that alley, I was simply destroyed.

I became another man, the one the villagers would have expected me to grow up to be. And I went home, sick and silent, malleable, simple, just the way he wanted me to be.

Again the underlining was deep and cutting, almost tearing the paper, and the anger and aggression was alive on the page. I put my head down on Angel's silky fur. She turned and licked my face, compassionately, her big eyes liquid and soft, almost as if she could feel my grief.

Was Nat referring to his father? Had that cruel, cold man—the kind of man who could ignore his wife's embarrassment and loss of dignity as he wheeled her around in a flimsy nightgown, the kind of man who could throw a beautiful dog into the arms of strangers—been his own son's tormentor? Had the cavernous walls of the bridgeman's cottage led inevitably to the Den of Nathaniel's hell?

Rejection from everyone, including his own parents, had turned a confused little boy into a sadistic, twisted man who needed to have power and degradation to feel sexually fulfilled. In some ways, it seemed a miracle, even a gift, that he had not turned to the rape and murder of women. And although I did not consider an animal's life less important than a human's, at the moment, my head buried in this loving little dog's fur, I could not feel the difference. Nat had indulged in torture and rape of helpless animals. I could not imagine the life those beasts had had to endure. I could not imagine that they could have lived very long in those conditions. Had Nat continued his depraved lifestyle here in Burchill? Was his father part of it? Did we have our own Den here in this sleepy, unsuspecting community?

I knew about the land that he owned just north of Burchill. It is a perfect place for his operation. Surrounded by a huge bush of trees, it's accessible only through a dirt road that you can barely see from the road. He makes a great deal of money, much of which he has shared with me, and which I have taken. Blood money, yes, but in my perverse way, I have spent it in contributions to those organizations that fight what I have helped to create and maintain. Ironic, twisted of course, but that is who I am. I am a complete persona now.

It seems that all my life I have been condemned to wear a mask that prevents people from seeing the real me. Even my parents did not love or accept me. They gave me only punishment and rebuke. I have always thought that their reaction to me was because of my great ugliness. I have never blamed them. Taunted and jeered as a child, told I should join a circus, I retreated, always avoiding looking glasses and store windows and the mirror of another human being's eye. Inside, behind the mask, is a sensitive, warm, affectionate boy now man, longing to be held and loved and respected. I had never met anyone who could look beyond my hideous exterior, until SHE came to Burchill. Would everything have been different if only I had seen that she might enter my life?

Some time ago, he allowed me to burn the pictures. By then, and perhaps all along, he knew that they were not the rope that tied me to this life. He knew that instead, it was my own desires. Even now, I can remember each movement, each and every time. I picture my actions as though I am watching a film, a filthy, pornographic movie about someone beneath contempt.

Once I have provided my parents with food and helped with the bridge, I lock the door of my rooms at the back of our house and draw all the draperies. I put on my old, loose jeans and the red hunting jacket.

Then, slowly and awkwardly, my fingers numb and stiff, I eat my simple meal. I eat at a deliberately slow pace, always with a small glass of sherry. (Someone once told me that sherry was too delicate a drink for me, so I drink it purposely.) Already the feeling has control. Any love or sensitivity I have is replaced by animosity, an odious venom. I coldly, calculatingly, plan what I will do this time.

As soon as darkness sets, and my parents are asleep in their side of the house, I slip out the back door and drag my bicycle out of the shed. In the silence and under cover of the trees, I take the path across the country, from the yard through the woods, through the cornfields, to our compound. Leaning the bike against the cottage, I make my way to the barn.

The animals make soft snuffling sounds, rubbing against me, sniffing for their dinner. I can feel their heat in the twilight, smell their musty fur. Rubbing gently against each nose, warm and wet, I feed them carefully. When this is done, I choose the one I want, the pony, one of the goats, or the lovely collie.

The feeling, the hatred, floats in my chest. Eyes inert, blank with a frigid stare, I take whatever weapon is handy and methodically beat the animal, usually on the buttocks and belly, where the wounds will not easily be seen. All the time I speak to them quietly, obscenely, using words I heard while wandering away from Burchill. Filth, perversion, despising all spills from my lips.

The animal usually whimpers or cries softly, terrified by years of fear into submission. Since those long ago days when I first brought them to this prison camp, they have been too frightened to move away or retaliate. Or perhaps they know somehow that, despite their degradations on a weekly basis, their plight is better than the others'.

When it is over, when the feeling is gone, I feel weak and dizzy. I drag the animal back into the cages, leaving it whining softly in the darkness.

Then I prepare the compound for the arrival of more monsters like me, those who share my proclivities, who for their own twisted reasons seek to debase and abuse, who are willing to pay anything to be able to live out their disgusting fantasies.

Although I have changed my ways, though I myself have left that life, I cannot forgive myself, just as she would never forgive me if she ever knew. She thinks I am someone I am not. My purpose in life now is to be the person she believes I am. Yet I remember all those nights of my past, all the nights of my present as I continue to facilitate others in spewing out their evil, and I wonder if I can hide from her well enough to sustain her affection and respect.

These days, each dawn I mourn over my nights, because she is there in the light of the sun. Miracles happen each time I see her, talk to her, sometimes touch her. She doesn't appear to care that I am ugly. She doesn't think I'm stupid. She looks right into my eyes and talks to me, asks me questions, seeks my advice. She doesn't know the dark side of me. She likes me for this mask, I know this. The mask I wear now is far too ingrained, too important, to let slip. But she has given me something that I never thought possible. She has given me hope.

Hope that perhaps others could look beyond and see another me. Would someone be able to touch me without shuddering with revulsion? Would someone else be able to look into my eyes and see love or affection or intelligence or kindness? Would they be able to see past the lumps and imperfections and scars to what had begun as pure, soft, needy, loving? Is she perhaps the someone for me in this world, someone to love me, hold me, heal me? Or will her acceptance, will the things she has taught me and the lessons she still has to impart to me, at least lead me to a relationship at long last?

It is for this hope that I must talk with him, tell him it is over. I can no longer live this way. I must find some way to persuade him that it must stop. I have some plans. I need to feed his greed for money.

The sun had drenched the room in gold, warm on my face and arms. I looked up into a blue and yellow day, fresh and sweet after the rain, the lake calm, the trees full and free. The darkness of the words on these pages was completely anathema to the life all around me.

I turned the page and found the crude map, more a series of squiggles and lines than anything precise. Beyond that, there were several more pages of writing. But I was almost dizzy with the emotional turmoil. I needed sleep. Most of all, I needed Langford Taylor.

CHAPTER 14

I remembered with a start that I had shared none of this with Will. Over the last four years together, we had kept nothing back from each other—nothing of the present, at least. Our agreement to keep secret some parts of the twenty years before that was unspoken, but had helped to leave the past behind. I knew right now, though, that I couldn't share what had happened with Nathaniel Ryeburn with anyone. I wasn't sure that I could express my feelings, even with Langford. I wasn't even certain of the words I would use. So I tucked the diary in the magazine holder next to the sofa. Lang never reads magazines and would not in a million years riffle through.

I tucked my nightgown around me and flew quickly and quietly up the stairs, Angel at my heels, and slid into the warm bed. As if she knew my intentions, the little dog settled on the carpet and promptly, discreetly, closed her eyes. Langford Taylor turned warmly in sleep, automatically putting out his arms to encircle me. Very soon he was wide awake and I forgot the ugliness of Nathaniel Ryeburn's life in the complete expression of love.

Everything was out of sync. Here I was, sleeping late on a Tuesday in June when I should have been crazily busy at work, finishing reading and signing report cards, completing schedules for September, ensuring class lists for the coming year were correct and so on. Although I slept until ten that morning, I was still tired when I got up, fatigue that didn't just have to do with a failed night's sleep. Everything that had happened, everything I had read and lived through that writer's eyes, seemed like a dream, a nightmare.

I stumbled sleepily into the kitchen, hungrily pouring myself a coffee from the pot Will had made earlier, willing the caffeine to give me a clear head. My husband had quietly gone to his studio. I could vaguely see the top of his head from the window. I was glad he could still work, yet envious at the same time. He had the capacity to categorize events and feelings much more readily than I.

After a quick breakfast, I went upstairs and had a long, hot shower, which didn't seem to help my muddled state of mind. I knew there were so many things I should be doing. I couldn't just ignore my work. I had to gain control of my mind. The only way to do that, I concluded finally, was just to sit down at my desk and start, which is exactly what I did. Thus by early afternoon, when Will came in from his painting, I was much brighter, more satisfied, because I had accomplished several tasks.

We had lunch outside in the sunshine, munching on fresh egg salad sandwiches and carrot sticks, watching birds gather on the shore of the lake. It was a perfect June day, only a few days away from official summer. The air was clear and fresh. White clouds twisted into cartoon shapes over the blue of the sky.

The diary seemed to be part of a terrible movie I'd just watched or a fictional novel I'd been sorry I'd purchased. Consumed in my mind by the work of the school for which I was responsible, I mulled over all those details instead. I refused to stop to consider what I should do with Nathaniel Ryeburn's writings. By now I couldn't deny that it could very well have something to reveal about Nat's death. I didn't make a firm decision to continue the secrecy. I just postponed thinking about it until later. It would prove to be a very wrong move.

Will and Angel decided to accompany me to Ottawa for the special Board meeting. We'd better get her used to traveling, Will had pointed out, and I don't want you driving all the way back in the dark by yourself. I shuddered at the thought and tucked myself under his arms again, thankful for the millionth time for his love and his presence. We started our small journey early, packing a picnic dinner for all three of us, planning to stop by the Ottawa River Park that we loved. We knew dogs were allowed to run fairly free there, having been the recipients of many unwanted visitors to our picnics in the past. The day continued its perfect weather pattern, supporting our plans, and my mind did not even once turn to Nat's diary until after the Board meeting.

I was well prepared, able to answer the questions of the Board members, for once grateful that I did not have to make all the decisions on my own. As seemed to be normal for that group, the conversations strayed everywhere, from comments on violence in society at large to security in our schools. There were several reporters on hand, ensuring some grandstanding by some of the elected officials.

Eventually, however, a plan was presented and voted upon. My little Burchill Public School would remain closed, a premature graduation for all. Next week, a day or two would be set for parents to pick up report cards at a place to be determined by the principal. The Grade 8 Graduation ceremony was to take place in the fall, at a date to be, again, determined by the principal. In addition, I was requested to create a newsletter that would tie up loose ends, explain the situation as far as I was able, and to cooperate with the Ontario Provincial Police. Not a problem with the plans at all, I thought.

I had left Langford and Angel for two hours while the Trustees ruminated and decided and was anxious to ensure they were all right. As I approached the park, I was caught by the tableau in front of me. Langford and Angel Taylor were silhouetted in the setting sun, surrounded by a group of three little children and their parents. The kids were throwing a ball back and forth, Angel skipping happily to scoop it up, sometimes delighting them with an upright begging posture, almost dancing on her hind legs in her excitement. Her fur glistened golden red and I could imagine the shine of her huge brown eyes. The children's parents even clapped occasionally.

Will was angled toward Angel and the children, his whole posture relaxed and happy, completely entertained by the antics of the little ones and the dog. I felt a pang in my chest, tears staining my eyes, as I thought suddenly of the lost opportunity for this wonderful man to be a father. His loving arms would never encircle a little one, except perhaps as a friend or an uncle. He would never be able to sit a little person on his knee and read to them before bed. We had both been cheated of this gift by a hideous mistake, and there wasn't even anyone on whom we could take out our anger.

Now I thought of Nathaniel, of how he had chosen such innocents who could never speak out, making them the targets of his anger and disappointment and hatred. At least we had each other, Langford and I. At least we led decent lives filled with love and forgiveness, not resentment and violence.

I blinked away the tears and headed toward my husband and our little dog, my spirits once again elevated. Children would always be a part of our lives in other ways besides parenthood. We spent a few more minutes in the park, watching the sun dissolve into the horizon, until the evening chill reminded us of our drive home.

It was very dark by the time we turned onto the softly lit streets of

Burchill. Everything was quiet, as always. The bridge remained closed and still. People had gone into their homes and turned out most of their lights. Occasionally we could see one or two televisions flickering in our neighbours' windows, but for the most part, Burchill was asleep.

Langford and I were unaware of anything amiss until we opened the front door and Angel began to bark furiously. It was then that we saw the odd shapes in the living room, signalling that something was terribly wrong.

CHAPTER 15

We stepped cautiously into our home, Angel in front, barking and snarling, Will behind her, and myself taking up the rear. We were not thinking about intruders, really. I don't know what we thought as we imprudently walked onto the scene. It was not until Langford's shoe crunched on some glass that we panicked and backed out the front door, shocked and chilled, staring at one another in the dark, unable to speak or act. Suddenly the door slammed shut with the wind and we raced back to the car, terrified, the dog at our heels. We locked all four doors and got on the cell phone to Edgar.

Although it took him only five minutes, it seemed an eternity to us, sitting locked in the car, the dog whining and snarling by turns, our eyes frantically searching the house and the yard for any sign of human interference. Until Ed pulled into the yard, Will and I had not said a word. Now we both bombarded him with our story, and what we thought we had seen in our living room.

Edgar went with us to the front door, then made us stay back while he cautiously stepped into the living room. In a moment, he asked Langford to come and flip the light switch. My husband did so. Angel and I stayed behind both men, still shivering with fright. The sight of the living room did nothing to calm our nerves.

Everything had been turned upside down. The sofa lay on its side, stuffing pierced and pulled like an old doll. Cushions had been sliced and strewn everywhere. Drawers from both end tables had been yanked out and papers thrown all around. The lamps had been smashed on the hardwood floor. Magazines were torn and dispersed as if a small child had enjoyed ripping and tossing what could not be read. I let out a cry of dismay and Will's arms encircled me immediately.

Angel careened wildly through the room, sniffing and barking and whining. Finally, Will reached over for her. We hugged her to us, while Edgar spoke into his cell phone, calling on Barry and Michael. He signalled us to follow him, flipping lights on as we went, carefully making our way through the rest of our house. One of the large glass windows at the side of the house was now shattered, a gaping hole darkened by the trees and the expanse of the night, giving clear entry and exit. The drapes curled in the night air, quiet now. The broken glass was the only testimony to the break-in. Someone had smashed the window in, entered the living room, and then begun to throw our belongings around.

The kitchen, the bedrooms, the family room, the basement—all were empty and untouched.

Barry and Michael, ruffled, sleepy, and concerned, did a thorough search after our cursory hunt for any intruders, writing notes and taking pictures as they went. After profuse thanks from Edgar and from us, they left, unusually quiet and subdued. The events of the last few days had shaken them.

"The vandal must have found what he was looking for in the living room," Edgar concluded, "or else he was interrupted. Either that, or this was just done to annoy you, though this seems a little extreme for a prank. Is there anything missing, Emily? Langford?"

We swept over the living room, trying to picture it as it had been. We stared at broken gifts and souvenirs, attempting to see if anything valuable was missing. Langford's paintings remained on the wall and his studio was still locked and safe. Magazines, papers, all there.

I knew, of course I did. No soft brown book in sight.

Obviously, Edgar muttered, this was pure vengeful vandalism, or the thief had been focused on one thing only, had found it.

I had to tell them. As soon as I began, the tears started to flow and I was suddenly weak and dizzy. Langford helped me to the kitchen and sat me down on a chair, brought me tea and tissue, but I could feel his anger in the set of his mouth, the distance in his touch, his utter silence. My guilt only made the tears flow harder. Eventually, with pauses for breath and sips of hot tea, the whole story stumbled out. I tried to explain my silence about the diary to protect what I thought at first would have been innocent ramblings from a simple man, but which had turned out to be the deeply sordid tale of a sad and terrifying life. The silence when I finished was thick with shock and disappointment, not only for Nat, but also for the storyteller.

Edgar stared at me, involuntarily shaking his head, trying very hard to keep the anger out of his voice. "Emily." Softly said, but even more menacing because of that sotto voce. "You have to know how this will look to the OPP. Anyone outside of Burchill will wonder what your part in all of this is. They'll wonder why you didn't turn that diary in right away."

I stared back at Edgar, unable to believe my ears. I had not expected this line of thinking. "Ed," I croaked, then cleared my throat. "How can you think that way?"

"Because he's a police officer, Emily." Langford stood at the kitchen counter, his arms folded. "You must see how it might look to outsiders."

Unable to look at my husband, I lowered my head into my hands, trying to control my emotions. My body had begun a strange inward tremble, as if my blood and muscles were being shaken from the inside out. "Okay. But right now, it's just us. And someone has somehow found out that I had Nat's diary. They have broken into our home and stolen it. The diary must be very significant. I don't know if everything in there is true. I find it hard to believe that the Nathaniel Ryeburn we knew is the monster on those pages, but it seems that someone wanted him dead. They must also have killed the pony to vacate the school and have more time to search the school for the diary. Again, we're back to IT."

Edgar tapped his fingers on the table. "I think you're right. We have no way of knowing how much more Nat was about to say, or how long ago he wrote the diary. But it sounds like Nathaniel was about ready to blow the whistle and maybe, just maybe, he had started to put the pressure on this partner of his. The partner decides to kill Nat. He knows about the diary somehow. Can't find it, so he kills the pony to ensure the vacating of the school. That way he can spend time searching."

"Or she."

"No time for feminism, Emily." At least Edgar could still smile at me. "But you got to the diary first. How did he know that? He could have seen you reading in your living room, I suppose. Or maybe he just knew that Nat was close to you and made a lucky guess. Either way, someone has been watching you, Emily."

A shiver went down my spine. I had let evil into our house. Yet instead of feeling depressed and upset, I was suddenly angry. "We have to find out who did this, Edgar. I think we'll have our murderer as well. A strong suspect is Nat's own father, I'm afraid to say. His mother's in a wheelchair, so that counts her out. However, Mr. Ryeburn—not only is he a strange, menacing man, he spent a long time abusing Nathaniel. And from what I remember in Nat's writings, it indicated pretty strongly that he could be this mysterious partner."

"He did bring us Angel, though. Why would he come to our house with a dog? Wouldn't that start us thinking?" I was glad to hear Langford's voice. He must be thawing, I hoped.

"I suppose so. But maybe it was one way of watching me. Or maybe his wife truly did insist. Maybe SHE was trying to send us a message."

Edgar tapped the table again, nervously, fidgeting, unable to decide what to do. "OK, listen. Don't do anything stupid. Sit tight. I appreciate your thinking about this, but Emily, do not get involved. I will have to consult with some of the Ottawa people tomorrow for sure. But I'll start with someone I know and trust, to see what they think I should do." He heaved a huge sigh and stood up. "Emily, I wish you'd done this differently, but I do understand. I know why Nat respected and admired you, and you wanted to protect his privacy. You couldn't have known what you'd find." He patted my hand, looking up at Langford, as if sensing that he was still angry. "However, once you did know, I wish you'd trusted me enough to tell me."

"It was nothing to do with trust or lack of, Ed," I protested, knowing Will was hearing me too. "I just couldn't believe what I was reading. I didn't honestly know if it really was Nat or just somebody else with a sick sense of humour. And until last night, I wasn't positive it could have anything to do with Nat's murder." I turned to face Will. "But you're right. I should have told you from the beginning what I found in the basement that day."

Edgar patted my hand again. "Let's get you safe for now. I'll help you board up the window, Langford."

Using leftover wood still stocked in our garage from our most recent renovations, Edgar and Langford nailed us in tightly and, I thought, even more safely than before. Their hammering seemed to ring out over the calm, dark lake, and I worried about everyone hearing and being more frightened than they probably were. But I couldn't move. I sat still and frozen at the table, my mind slow and empty.

Eventually Edgar came in to say good-bye. He'd be in touch tomorrow. I simply nodded without comment, too miserable to reply as he disappeared out the door.

"Emily..."

"I know, I know. Please, Will. Don't say anything right now. I know I was wrong. But I can't deal with that at this moment. Please just wait until I can talk about it. Please." I put my head on my arms, expecting Will to walk away at my angry outburst. He didn't, though. Instead he leaned over, his head next to mine, his long hands covering mine.

"It's okay," he whispered. "I was just scared and worried. We'll work this out together. Let's go to bed and hold each other, darling. We'll clean up tomorrow and arrange for a new window and all that when we can see the light of day." And so once again, I slept in Will's arms, gathering strength in his touch and support, until we woke to the early sunlight and Angel's wet kisses.

CHAPTER 16

There seemed to be an unspoken bond created during the night, which held us up that day. Arranging for the replacement of the window, cleaning up the debris from the vandalism, writing the newsletter for the school, all of it we accomplished together, standing close by one another, our bodies touching gently and often. Our little dog watched us carefully, as if afraid to leave us on our own. Strength began to pour back into my soul and mind.

Edgar rang the doorbell about 2:30, just as the window company had begun their task. The living room had been cleared of debris and vacuumed twice. All broken objects had been tossed away. No remembrance of the vandalism remained other than the two heads stuck in the hole, hammering away any vestiges of broken glass, measuring and muttering to each other. My schoolwork had been accomplished. I had emailed the newsletter to the Education Centre, as well as a message to the staff.

Ed sat with Will and me in the kitchen. All three of us had a cold beer, our nerves needing sustenance.

"Ottawa isn't going to be happy. My contact says we need to let them know right away. Delaying will just appear strange. I will call when I leave here. It may be a double standard, Em, but my friend thinks it will help enormously that you are the school principal. She doesn't think they'll seriously see you as some kind of suspect."

Will's hand tightened in mine. *Suspect.* I had never thought we'd hear these words again. I began to wish fervently that I had never told them about the diary. No one would have had a clue what was missing. Except whoever took it, I reminded myself. For once I decided to keep my mouth shut. I had learned the hard way how to harden my tell tale face—how to prevent every single emotion and thought from beaming right out of my eyes—but sometimes my mouth still got the better of me.

The beer tasted wonderful, so cold and bubbly and relaxing, that it called for another. Edgar didn't seem in any hurry to leave, nor did he appear to be worried about drinking on the job, so I threw a plate of crackers and cheese together and we went outside. The sky was once again perfect, the air fresh and warm without a trace of humidity. We sat on the large chairs at the edge of the lake, I dipping my feet in the water, and talked of Nathaniel, the school, about Burchill and what would happen now that our peace had been disturbed.

Edgar had some wonderful stories of past indiscretions by the ancestors of the town. He swore the tales were true, passed down orally by the villagers and their relatives. Not once did Edgar's phone ring to disturb our afternoon. Not once did he demonstrate the disappointment he must still feel toward me. We were interrupted only once when the workers came to tell us they'd finished the window and Will went to pay them.

Our little bay was a tiny cove cut into Ogeechee Lake almost as though it were an afterthought. The narrow section between the shores was not friendly to boats. On an afternoon like this one, you would think it was our own private beach. Rarely did people intrude on the peace, other than some of our neighbours who might walk this way for an occasional swim. You had to be Burchill-born to even want to swim here, though. Besides crossing through the mucky sand to the deeper areas, you had to wade through a web of weeds that brushed your arms and legs and grabbed at your toes. If you were courageous enough to get through this part though, you were rewarded with golden water that left your skin silky and your body replenished.

In the sunshine on this day, I was content to lie back in my chair, sipping on beer, joining in pleasant conversation, and watch the wind tease the water into little pools or the sunlight dancing on the brown curves of the lake. Once in a while a little fish would jump or a water spider would sprint over the surface. I could almost forget Nathaniel Ryeburn had lived and died in violence.

Complete forgetting was not to be, however. As Edgar parted company to walk through the village to his office, he put his hand on my shoulder. "Emily, I'll call to let you know what Ottawa wants me to do. You two aren't planning to go anywhere tonight, are you?"

I shivered, wrapping my arms around myself. Edgar had no idea how devastating his innocent words were to my bruised heart and ragged memory. "Nope, definitely not. We're spending a quiet evening at home. If they want to see me tomorrow, that's not a problem either. I've got some schoolwork to do and some parents to call. Other than that, well, I'm kind of on an early vacation, as you know."

He nodded briefly and went on his way. I watched his tall, lumbering figure cover the ground in quick, smooth strides until he disappeared behind the house. Will came over and put his arms around me.

I buried my head in his shirt, smelling his aftershave and the salt of his perspiration. "I'm so sorry, my darling."

"It's all right, Em. When I think about it, I can understand what you did completely. After all, you had no idea what you would find in that diary. You couldn't have ever guessed what lay inside Nathaniel Ryeburn." His voice was soft in my ear, as comforting as the lap of the water on the shore. "Let's go upstairs and forget about all of this for a while."

We walked hand in hand upstairs, Angel trailing at our feet only until the first step, whereupon she turned toward the kitchen, undoubtedly to scout out the food in her dish. We took off our clothes without ceremony and climbed into comfortable silky sheets, the duvet thrown over the foot of the bed.

I felt sorry for those who, like Nathaniel Ryeburn, never feel the touch of real love. On that afternoon, Will's fingers traced every line of my body, a map he was familiar with yet managed to infuse with the enthusiasm of a new explorer. His lips were soft and gentle, nudging me to the oblivion of excitement, tingling everywhere with pleasure, unable to think any dark thoughts. In fact, I had no thoughts at all. I became physical only. Every part of me invested in response to his movements, his touches, his kisses.

In turn, I hand painted his body with the tips of my fingers, going over the golden and silver hairs that covered his chest and arms and legs. We gave each other the gift of this touching for a long time before we were unable to hold back the rush of desire, crushing together as if we could melt into one being. When we were completely connected, Will used his hips and his hands to bring me to an explosion so profound that I cried out. Wave after wave consumed me as I felt him pour into me, shuddering together. Our bodies were sheathed in sweat but still we clung to one another, not wanting to separate.

The late afternoon sun kept us warm and comforted as we pulled apart, hands still linked, each now in our different worlds with our own thoughts. I was to be forever grateful for this lovemaking. I believed it kept me sane throughout the next few days of fear and horror. The telephone's strident ring was what began everything all over again.

CHAPTER 17

Constables Petapiece and Ducek sat in Edgar's office at the back of the OPP station. Once again, the traditional male/female roles had been assumed. Petapiece sat with a notebook as if she were a secretary, while Ducek sat behind the desk, his large white hands spread over the dark wood as if attempting to display the age-old colors of good and bad. They had lost their sympathy for the poor woman who'd found a dead body in her sacred space. They were now wondering if they had a clever liar in front of them.

Their stance annoyed me. I could feel my heart beginning to pound until I realized that this was likely their intention. I took several shallow but thorough breaths, straightened my skirt, and sat down. Edgar sat several feet away in his own chair. Not too close, I noticed, but enough for support to be implied. Will had insisted on being present. As a result of all the people in the room, Edgar's small office was cramped and hot. I could feel the sweat begin to crawl down my back.

"We have a few further questions, Mrs. Taylor, as you can probably imagine."

I simply nodded, remembering not to reply when unnecessary. I had learned my lessons well. "Please tell us about this diary." He said the word as though it were something filthy. Little knowing, I presumed, just how right he was.

As precisely as I could, I explained about finding the diary and Nathaniel's papers. I told them he'd made me promise to keep the stash secret. Until I read the diary, I'd had no idea of the horrors they contained. With as much detail as I could, I told them what secrets the diary had revealed. I told them about the brutality toward animals, the mysterious partner and the shadowy but unnamed 'business' in which Nat had been reluctantly involved. Throughout the story, Ducek's eyes never left mine, other than when I shifted to Will's. Whenever it seemed that somehow my husband was being drawn into the discussion, I deliberately avoided looking in his direction at all.

There was a deep silence in the room when I'd finished. Only the sound of Petapiece's scribbling to catch up with the narration interrupted the silence. I could hear the distant voices of the villagers, the occasional passing of a car, some laughter thrown in our direction by the breeze. Life carried on as usual outside these doors. I felt my body shiver in anticipation of life never being normal again in our side of Burchill.

"You can see how this looks to outsiders, Emily," Constable Ducek said softly. I wondered if he were including himself and his partner as outsiders or not. "You have admitted to stealing some papers from the scene of the crime."

"It's my school." I couldn't help the interruption. My words sounded haughty and defensive even to my ears.

"It's also currently the scene of a crime," he retorted, appropriately haughty and defensive in return. "Now someone has broken into your house and removed the evidence that might have assisted us in solving this crime. Again, to an outsider, it might look as though you are only telling us about the diary because it's now in someone else's hands. Maybe you were, and still are, trying to obstruct justice because you are the one who is responsible for Mr. Ryeburn's death." He held up his hand to withstand both my and Will's sputtering. "I know, that doesn't seem to make sense to any of us here, but *if* you were guilty of murder, you might be doing illogical things to cover up. Not that any one of us HERE thinks you are capable of such an act."

I wrapped my arms around myself, deliberately not looking at or touching my husband. It seemed as though history were about to repeat itself. Only this time, I was sitting in the chair of the accused. Though Ducek's last words were, I assumed, meant to be reassuring, I couldn't help but hear a touch of sarcasm, whether or not it was real.

Now Petapiece spoke, in soft tones that must've meant she was the good cop. "Mrs. Taylor, was there anything in the diary which might lead you to suggest someone who should be questioned again?"

I thought about that for a few moments, hesitating to put someone else in the spotlight. "I told you about how he mentioned that he was forced to join into some kind of partnership because there were some pictures that this person had. Nat feared the man would tell his mother everything. I thought at the time that maybe he was referring to his own father. Maybe he said his partner was one of the elite in Burchill because of his father's station as the bridgeman. But then I couldn't imagine Walter Ryeburn doing something like that to his own child."

Yet I remembered the scene with his wife, his cheerful and purposeful shaming of her in front of us. I thought of the murderous look he had given me when he brought Angel into our lives. I wondered, but didn't say any of this aloud.

Constable Ducek tapped his fingers on the desk, lost in thought. Will reached out and deliberately hung onto my hand. *I am connected to you. Don't shut me out*, he was saying. I squeezed back.

"Was there any hint about where this business is located?"

I shook my head. "Nothing clear, at least to the point I'd reached when the diary disappeared. He just said it was land outside of Burchill." Why didn't I tell them about the meagre details, the map? To this day, I don't really know. I only know that I was frightened and upset, that my mind was muddled, that I felt like a suspect.

The Constables gave each other a look, which appeared to speak volumes to one another.

"Okay, Emily, I guess that's it for now," Constable Ducek said. "As they say in the movies, just don't leave town, huh? We may have to pick at your memory of the diary in case we want to follow up. In the meantime, we'll question Mr. Ryeburn." He stood up and reached for my hand to shake it. "I do appreciate the fact that you finally told us about the diary and that you've shared its contents readily. I understand that you may have had no idea what you were taking when you removed the diary. But you must also understand that, should this investigation lead in any direction toward you," he shifted his gaze to Will, "or to Mr. Taylor, the fact that you removed it may be seen as a criminal act. That is, if it looks like obstruction of justice, or a cover-up for someone else, or any number of scenarios. I'm sure you appreciate the gravity of what I am telling you."

Constable Petapiece added, "As well, please ensure that everything you've told us here is kept strictly confidential."

I shook their hands and stood as well, nodding my head, not trusting myself to speak. Will shook hands too, saying good-bye warmly to Edgar, and we left. Out on the sidewalk, I let the trembling loose. Will wrapped his arms around me and hurried me to the car. We had no desire to walk around Burchill. The sunshine and clear air of a beautiful late spring afternoon had no effect on our dark mood. We both felt as if we had been plunged back into a hell that we had assumed was gone forever.

CHAPTER 18

When we arrived back home, we found another surprise waiting for us. Bill and Marjory Percival sat on the swing on the front porch, bundles of white foam packages resting on their knees. Bill stood up and smiled as we approached.

"Emily, Langford, hello! We thought you might need some sustenance. And don't worry, if you don't want company, Marj and I can disappear immediately."

I looked up at Will and we both seemed to have the same thought. Distraction and good food might prove an excellent antidote. I took some of the packages and put my arm around Marjory's waist. "This is wonderful, you guys. How did you know what we needed?"

"What about the Inn?"

"You are a thoughtful bunny, Langford. Don't worry, we've got good employees," Marj said, turning to smile up at my husband. "And we are close by!"

The evening was wonderful, especially after the angst of that afternoon's events. Marj and Bill had cooked up fabulous angel hair pasta, with a rose sauce, and thrown in all kinds of grilled vegetables and shrimp. Their famous house salad tasted as good as in the restaurant, accompanied by as many buns and butter as they had been able to carry.

We served bottles of our favourite wine until everything was funny and the laughter was loud and long. Bill told marvellous stories about bumbling reporters who had gone on wild goose chases all over the county. Television news personalities sat in the restaurant expecting everyone to recognize them and no one did. He regaled us with colourful tales about the villagers' hilarious responses to the intruders to Burchill. Although the topic was Nathaniel, it really wasn't. Bill and Marjory asked no questions, did not refer to the murder of the pony, and shared only the funny side effects of the invasion of our little town.

By the time they left, after coffee, liqueurs, and Marj's incredible white chocolate mousse cake, we were more than slightly drunk, very full, and extremely sleepy. Will and I snatched off our clothes as soon as the doors were locked and tumbled into bed, grateful to our friends for an evening of laughter amid our own private chaos.

Although we'd been in Burchill for two years, we hadn't made many friends. May and Alain Reneaux had been our first 'couples' contact, as a result of my working, and now friendly, relationship with May. On one occasion, May and Alain had invited Marjory and Bill to dinner as well.

Once, all six of us had gone out on a boat cruise. Each time had been fun and interesting, with no lulls in conversation. It was nice to know that Marj and Bill felt comfortable enough to surprise us with dinner and a visit.

Late the next morning, I was sitting at the table feeling the effects of last night's frivolity when Edgar knocked at the door. He took one look at me and said, "Oh my God, Emily, this whole thing is ruining our relationship! Every time you look at me now it's obvious that you feel tense. I miss your smile! I can't wait until things get back to normal."

I didn't have the heart to tell him that, from my experience, nothing ever did get back to normal. I just grabbed his hand and pulled him into the kitchen, pouring his coffee as he sat, trying to smile.

"I've been spoiled, Emily. Burchill is such a quiet place. Nothing remotely like this has ever happened to anyone in our little town. So I have to admit that the big bad policeman is having trouble handling it." He sipped gratefully at the coffee, his kind eyes wrinkled and troubled.

"Ed, as far as I'm concerned, you're handling it very well. I know the pressure you must be getting from Ottawa. They don't know any of us. My actions haven't exactly been the kind you can vouch for one hundred per cent. You're doing well considering everything." I put a plate of tea biscuits in front of him. We nibbled and sipped in silence for a moment and I struggled to remove the cobwebs, as well as a post-high depression, from my head.

"I'm not here with good news, Emily. In fact, I am probably just about an hour ahead of the Ottawa police." He paused, a long agonizing time it felt to me. I just barely held back from yelling at him to hurry up and tell me, no don't tell me, go away, I don't want to hear it.

Finally, "Walter Ryeburn appears to be missing" was the last thing I expected him to say. My mouth literally dropped open. I was unable to utter anything as I struggled to draw in a shocked breath.

"His wife managed to call 911 sometime very early this morning. She said he'd stormed out right after the police questioned him. He had left Annie without means to take her medication or to get out of her wheelchair into the bed. By dawn she was in agonizing pain. She apparently had to slink to the floor and drag herself down the stairs to a telephone. They only have one goddamned phone in that whole place. She's got a couple of broken ribs and a few bruises on her face. Annie wouldn't confirm she'd received them when she got out of the wheelchair or perhaps fell down the steps. Who the hell knows what Walter Ryeburn does in his own home? By the sounds of his poor screwed up son, Walter's a hell of a guy."

I took another sip of coffee to clear my throat from some obstruction that had suddenly cut off speech. "Edgar, this is—what *is* this?"

He shook his head. "I have no idea, Emily. It looks to me as though Walter Ryeburn is totally involved in his own son's death. I can't think of any other explanation. Ottawa has other thoughts, I believe. They are still suspicious of our own school principal and her husband for some reason." He looked me directly in the eyes. "I don't understand why they're targeting you and Langford. But that's the way it seems to me. They're coming over to question you on your whereabouts of last evening. They certainly don't trust me to do it properly. I shouldn't even be here and I certainly shouldn't be telling you any of this." A ragged breath sounded through his lips. "They think that because you fingered Walter, and now he's missing, that somehow you and Langford are involved in what happened. Emily, is there something I don't know?"

For a fleeting moment I did think of telling Edgar everything. This kind, thoughtful man who handled a tough job with integrity, fairness and feeling. Didn't he deserve the whole truth about why Ottawa might be interested in us? Yet I did not know for sure that Ottawa *was* 'targeting' us. Even if they were, it wasn't necessarily because of my husband's past. I hadn't known Edgar Brennan long. I had really no idea if this was the real Ed or if it was a technique he was using. I had reason to be suspicious of law enforcement. Looking back, as bad as events became, everything would surely have been worse had I given in to my desire to confide in Edgar. So I shook my head, fed the police officer more biscuits, and finished the visit with inconsequential chatter.

Thus when the OPP officers arrived at our home and asked to interview me, it was William (aka Langford Taylor), who sat by my side in a reverse parody of twenty-four years before. Little did the interviewers know that their interrogation was so mild in comparison that, if I'd had anything to hide, I would have had no trouble lying or exaggerating the truth. I'd had much greater, more gruelling, practice in the past. We didn't ask for a lawyer to be present, because I was not being accused of a crime, or so they told me. They didn't mention Will's past, but by law they were unable to bring it into the conversation anyway. To me, it floated there. I was convinced that someone must have discovered what happened in Vancouver. Our past collared the conversation orange and red and suspicious.

I answered their questions as truthfully as I could. There was really very little to tell. Nathaniel Ryeburn had hidden a dark, vicious life under one that could only be seen as routine and dull. Until reading his journal, I'd had no inkling of the persona behind my simple caretaker. I had been denied the chance to read the part of the journal that might have given detailed clues as to who might have killed him and his pony. It was clear that Walter Ryeburn was suspect number one, but only because of his disappearance. Constables Ducek and Petapiece also hinted very strongly that Walter might be a victim of the same clever killer or killers. Anything I could remember might help.

Whether real or imagined, I saw the doubt in their faces. Were they seeing two clever killers sitting in their lovely, middle-class living room, hiding as deeply as Nathaniel Ryeburn had, their involvement in criminal activity and their lust for power so strong they would kill? Had I murdered Nat in the school and then attempted to look like the innocent principal stumbling upon a gruesome sight? What better explanation for the missing gun, the missing diary, the pony by my office, the father now gone after I led the police to his doorway? Here were two people who had a deep secret and hid it well. Our masks of respectability and innocence were perfectly in place in this village. Had the Ryeburns threatened that? I could almost hear the other questions behind the ones I was asked out loud.

That night Will and I lay in bed, fingers touching, each lost in our own thoughts. It was impossible not to be frightened. We had been innocently accused and found wanting before. Would it happen again?

Where was Walter Ryeburn?

Is your real name William? Are you a convicted criminal? Tell us about your past, Mr. Taylor. Mrs. Taylor, where were you last night? Are you aware that Mr. Ryeburn had a crush on you? Don't you know that all his words in the diary were directed at you? Didn't you realize that he had a sexual fantasy about you, Mrs. Taylor? Did you taunt him by showering at the school every morning? I think we'd better arrest your husband and take him downtown for questioning. Call the lawyer, honey. I never showed this to nobody. You won't tell, will you? Angel, what's the matter? Why are you crying? If anythin' ever happens, Mrs. Emily, would you get rid of this here stuff for me? Wouldn't want nobody readin' my personal stuff, doncha know? Killing, cutting, playing, taking everything apart and putting it back together if I feel like it. Total, complete, control. Transcending them and me and our earthly bodies and joining a dance of destruction. The pony is dripping blood all over the carpet.

    I awoke several times, shivering and perspiring. Will's hand reached out for me in his sleep, comforting me even from his subconscious. My dreams continued to be a tangled mix of present and past, of horror and pain, of degradation and hidden psychoses. By morning, I knew I had to do something or go mad waiting.

CHAPTER 19

I spent the day on school business ensuring parents would have year-end reports and interviews where necessary. I completed the class lists we'd begun earlier in the spring, readied all the other correspondence, and took them to May, who was also working from home.

Our visit was short, because she was watching me strangely. Her intuition and fair knowledge of the Emily Taylor I had let her see, were telling her that I was in some kind of trouble. She kept reaching out for my hand, squeezing my fingers, looking me straight in the eyes. Her kindness was almost too much for me to bear. I couldn't afford to cry right now.

I left her quickly, walking fast to wipe away any weakness, building up my strength for what I knew I had to do.

Will was still at work in the studio when I returned home. I went straight to the bedroom, Angel at my heels, and gathered the items I would need. Then I took the little dog in my arms, petting her and kissing her as if I would never see her again. I made a delicious dinner that night, avoiding the bottle of wine Will opened, and made love to my husband with every fibber of my body quivering with fear and regret. I didn't like lying to Will. I didn't want to disappoint him or make him angry. I knew he wouldn't agree with what I was about to do.

Long after dark, when Will and Angel were both snoring, I got up and headed for the bathroom. The little dog raised her head slightly, blinking at me, but I patted her head and she sighed, snuggling sleepily against Will once more. Slowly and silently, I dressed in the outfit I'd arranged earlier, left Will a note on the kitchen table, and locked my front door behind me.

It was a blue night, one just like the nights of my childhood at my uncle's cottage with its dark blue sky and white diamond stars. A light, warm breeze teased the tree branches, riffling my hair with gentle fingers. There was a deep silence at first, until my blocked city ears picked up the sounds of the night creatures. An owl murmured as she spotted a foolish mouse. Frogs cleared their throats. Waves licked the stones on the shore. Insects warned of my approach. No people lights invaded the darkness. Everyone I know was asleep, dreaming, perhaps innocently.

My footsteps were quiet and crunchy on the dirt and stones. My eyes began to open wider. I was able to see again as though a blindfold had been removed from around my head. Suddenly tree trunks were more than shadows and stealthy movements were visible in the grass ahead. Creatures unused to night disturbances raced away from my threatening presence. I couldn't help but jump now and then at their furtive escapes, but mostly I was unafraid, enveloped in the shawl of the warm night air.

The bridgeman's house was very dark and, even if I didn't know, I believe I would have been able to feel its emptiness. The blocks of the house were outlined in the blackness of the sunless sky and I wondered how people could have lived in such a cold, bleak building. I am somehow not surprised that this place had spawned a child whose inner self was twisted and evil.

The backyard was sinister but quiet as I poked around with my walking stick. It was a strong, smooth pole that I picked up years ago on a hike in the hills of the Rocky Mountains. It was with me now as both support and weapon. There seemed to be nothing for me in this former animal pen, this prison for pets. It was empty and sad, bereft of life.

I slip out the back door and drag my bicycle out of the shed. In the silence and under cover of the trees, I take the path across the country to our compound.

I remembered his words so clearly it was as if he spoke them in my ear. I headed straight for the shed, standing askew and cob webbed in the corner of the yard. Inside, the creatures of the night once again brushed against my hair and my collar, making me twist with fright, slapping at them unfairly, for it was I who had invaded their space. The animals that once stamped and cried and ate and lived in this little compound were now gone. Their smell still clung to the walls and the flooring. I could almost picture Angel and the pony looking up at Nathaniel with pleading eyes, the moon filling their irises with tears. I shook my head. It was not sentimentality that would carry me through this task.

The bicycle was old, built for a female, gangly and crooked as it leaned against the wall. I pulled it awkwardly out of the shed door, hearing the clangs and bangs in the silence as though a drum roll had begun in a deserted hall. I had not put on my flashlight, yet here I was making a noise that could wake the dead, I scolded myself, and then grinned perversely at the irony.

The gate in the fence around the yard was almost hidden by the shed. I had to push through ferns and overgrown bushes to get out. The foliage slapped back into place as if I'd never crossed this way, as if he had never been here night after night, on this very pathway, on this bicycle, pumping toward the obsession that held him so steadfastly that he wrought suffering on the very creatures that he adored. Reluctantly, after several awkward attempts, I had to leave my walking stick propped against the fence. There was no way I could steer this old bicycle and carry it with me. I stuck the flashlight in my pocket. I could use that as a weapon, I reasoned, and then cringed when I thought of Nathaniel and what he had done with such an instrument.

I couldn't help but be glad of my leather gloves, though my fingers perspired underneath them, but I didn't want to touch anything that he had touched. I tried not to think of his huge body perched on this bicycle, sweating and panting, excited by thoughts of the violence that he would perform on the poor animals in the darkness beyond.

I could not imagine anyone enjoying demeaning another creature, human or otherwise. It was so foreign to me. Sex has always meant love or affection, caring and mutual satisfaction. It had in turns been about fun or emotion or desire, not power, not debasement of another. I was somewhat naive, I guessed, but I was glad that life had not mangled my heart and thrust me into enjoying bringing harm to others. My thoughts were so intense, so inward, that I barely realized that I had found the path easily, that I was now bumping along the dirt mounds to a destination that remained in my mind as words on a page.

It is a perfect place for his operation. Surrounded by a huge bush of trees, it's accessible only through a dirt road that you can barely see from the highway.

I tried to picture the little map that had been scribbled onto the diary pages, but it was as if I were following the moon. I tried not to think as my shadow moved through the corn fields, the stalks just beginning to poke through the ground. I could see the tree forms in the distance, smell the damp earth, and feel the weight of the silence. Now and then my bike wheels got caught in roots twisted across the pathway, or a stone flew up and pinged against the frame, or a bird screamed at me from the field as it projected itself into the sky.

My skin was covered in goose pimples and my breath came fast, but I could not stop. I repeated my mission over and over to myself. *I must see the compound. I must find out where everything begins and ends, solve the mystery that has shaken my new life and threatened to plunge me back into hell. I must take this chance in order to put everything back the way it was.* And then suddenly, I was there.

The cottage looked so ordinary that at first I wondered if the path continued on the other side of this property to another one. It consisted of cedar shingles, a small front veranda, and several tiny windows with drawn curtains. The back porch seemed to have been built for a wheelchair, until I remembered with a surge of nausea the animals who'd probably had to track their way to the door. When I saw the chain link fence and the structures beyond, when I heard the whimpering of animals in the near distance, I knew I had come to the right place.

I remained behind the trees, listening, as if I could see through the dark and beyond the walls for human movement. If anyone were around, they would be asleep in the cottage, I assumed, or on guard near the compound. I decided to take the chance that the unseen, unknown person was asleep in the cottage. I propped the bicycle against a tree and used the light of the moon to guide me toward the structures shadowed by the edge of the forest to my right. I stumbled over roots and rocks a few times, but was always able to stay on my feet. As I approached the compound, it became more difficult to see, as the moon dipped over the trees and the rooftops.

The compound appeared to be a collection of small barns and sheds, about four buildings in all, with the largest very close to the tree line. I hunched over, some movie hero in my mind, and ran quickly from the safety of the trees to the doors of the barn. They were tall, wide and well sealed, obviously a delivery depot of some sort, for their size would allow large animals to pass through. I lifted the wooden bar and the door on my right swung noiselessly open.

CHAPTER 20

The odour hit me as soon as I slipped into the barn. My eyes began to sting and water. The air was so thick with urine and acidic smells that I felt as if I were pushing through liquid manure. I could hear the whimpering now and as I stepped closer, the pitiful yelping assaulted my ears. I forgot the danger I was in. Instead, I went from cage to cage, dazed, shocked, tears streaming down my face, my stomach twisted. If I'd had any food in the last few hours, I would have spilled their contents by now. My mouth and nose were choked with the sharp smells of feces and vomit and blood. Every breath I took was followed by a gag and a whimper of my own.

It seemed as though there were hundreds of cages. Many pairs of eyes gleamed at me from behind the netting, mouths open, panting, screeching, whimpering, crying. Even in the darkness I could see their matted fur, see the insect clouds burst from their bodies as the animals moved toward the human figure. They were crowded in on one another, but were too fatigued and weak to even bother pushing one another away. They simply leaned on each other, walked over inert figures, collapsed on each other. Many of the dogs appeared to be large with offspring, although their legs and faces were emaciated. Some of the bodies did not move and another acrid smell invaded my senses: death and dying, rotting flesh. I could not see them clearly. I knew you couldn't reach out to touch them or comfort them.

My sense of horror and futility propelled me forward. There was another door at the rear of the building and I clawed my way out into the night air.

Bent over, gasping, I inhaled as though coming up from under water. I gagged and vomited spittle, my mouth and nose still full of the overwhelming odour. At first I didn't think I could move, but soon I was stumbling toward the smaller building ahead. I was obsessed, moving stiffly and dazed. My mind did not register the danger in the cries emanating from the barn.

The next building was more shed than barn. The doors were as wide and large, but there was no peak. Its flat roof seemed to gleam in the moonlight as though made of tin. I pulled back the wooden slat and entered. Again my senses were assaulted with odours, but this time they were familiar—the heat of animals, the smell of wet fur, the sweetness of hay. There were several larger cages here, filled with pregnant animals and tiny newborns. The females looked at me silently, their eyes filled with defeat. Those puppies old enough to move around made small mewing sounds and then settled under the safety of their mother's fur. This prison was free from the death and despair, was cleaner, had trays of food and water. But this was stage one, and knowing where they might be stored in stage two made me want to vomit once more.

The third barn, similar in size to the first, was mostly empty. There was an assortment of animal stalls large enough for ponies, goats—a large collie?

Leaning the bike against the cottage, I make my way to the barn. The animals make soft snuffling sounds, rubbing against me, sniffing for their dinner. I can feel their heat in the twilight, smell their musty fur. Rubbing gently against each nose, warm and wet, I feed them carefully. When this is done, I choose the one I want, the pony, one of the goats, or the lovely collie.

I shivered at the memory of those words, at the reality of what faced me, and then I saw the dog in the corner of one of the stalls. Angel, I thought at first. She was the same color and size. Her aristocratic face was identical. But her emaciated body and spindly legs told a story not only of abuse but also of age. I realized that of course I was not looking at Angel. This was either her mother or an older sibling.

She lifted her beautiful head and growled at me, her teeth large and vicious, her eyes alight with fear and aggression. Angel's relative, twisted and abused. She strained against the chain that held her. I could see that she would have liked to tear me apart. I lifted my flashlight up to see more clearly. Suddenly, the dog turned away, her head hidden, her growls soft and helpless.

I was stunned by anger and grief, paralyzed by disgust and shock.

This must have been the site of Nathaniel's 'menagerie'. Now suddenly I was awake and aware. I heard the noise, saw the shadow behind me. I realized too late the danger of my descent into this prison.

CHAPTER 21

I came to consciousness slowly, aware at first only of the blinding pain in my head. My eyes felt glued shut. I had to struggle to force them to open. For some reason, I could not move my arms or legs, could not feel my fingers or toes. When my eyes finally opened, I had to shut them again quickly, groaning aloud at the severe pain that shot through me. I was flat on my back on a rough surface, my hands and feet bound. Incongruously, a shaft of moonlight was pointing itself right at my face. I waited for what seemed an eternity until the throbbing in my head began to subside a little, slowly opening my eyes a tiny slit at a time. Eventually I was able to look straight down my prone body, keeping my eyes hooded against the light.

I was lying on rough slats placed evenly between insulation, as though I were being held prisoner in an attic. The roof above was constructed from rough-hewn logs, through which the bright moon grinned. My hands were tied behind my back, painfully squashed between my body and one of the planks. My feet were crossed, with what looked like rope and tape melding them together. I felt choked by the tape across my mouth.

I knew that I could not move yet, rolling over would be both dangerous and painful. I began to think of my stupidity and tears rolled down my cheeks. It will do no good to cry, I told myself, but I couldn't help myself. The tears kept coming until my nose was clogged and I struggled to breathe. I was very close to panic when I heard voices below me. I couldn't hear every word. They spoke in soft tones, and quickly, as though they too were afraid.

"...two now...where the hell do you think this is leading?" The female's voice rose and I could hear the last sentence spoken in harsh anger.

I tried hard to concentrate. Certain the voice was familiar, but unable to think clearly. I squeezed my eyes shut again and focused on breathing, clearing my nose, calming my slamming heart. When I was able to take longer breaths through my nose and had filled my lungs with oxygen, I began to listen to the words more closely.

"We have to get out of here. She hasn't seen us yet." The male voice, distant, muffled—Walter Ryeburn?? Still no image came to mind.

"Just leave her here?" Female, high pitched with anxiety. Clogged by the space between us and the pain in my head, I just couldn't tell who it was. At least she seemed to care, I laughed to myself.

"I'll finish him off. He's almost there anyway. Someone will find her. Maybe we can do one of those anonymous telephone tips."

"I never thought it would be like this." Still high-pitched, almost hysterical.

"Let's get packed while it's still dark, come back and take him with us. We'll decide how to do it later." Nervous, shaky, gruff. Who...?

Some frantic sounds of people moving quickly, throwing aside unwanted items, boxing others, and then silence followed. I thought I could hear a car start up. I waited a long time, or so it seemed, and then twisted my neck to look at my surroundings. There had been so many shocks this terrible evening that I barely reacted to what I saw.

Curled in the opposite corner, his back to me, was a man. He was tied in the same fashion, but he had rolled over onto his side. I could see his white hair curled over the color of his drab brown jacket. His shoulders rose and fell in rhythmic breathing. He was either asleep or unconscious. It was that white curling hair that told me instantly who this was. Walter Ryeburn.

CHAPTER 22

I had to get out of there. It took me several rocks, rolls and falls to propel myself to a sitting position. My head pounded until my eyes showed me only black and grey vistas and I had to blink, breathe, blink, breathe, slowly for several minutes until my heartbeat slowed and my head cleared a little. Only then was I able to open my eyes fully again and focus on a solution to my dilemma.

There was something not too many people knew about me. I was almost double jointed, thanks to my long legs and short upper body. I could twist into different shapes, do somersaults easily, and bend so that I could tuck my legs against my chest and wiggle my arms up and over them. This last trick was one I hoped I never needed to use again, but it came in very handy on that night in the dusty attic of a puppy farm cottage.

Slowly, I wriggled my arms up and over, until they were in front of me. Once again I had to spend several minutes calming my breathing and my heart rate. I used my stiff, puffy fingers to pull the tape off my mouth, an excruciating feeling when it's done slowly, piece by piece. I drank in several draughts of air and coughed from deep in my chest and lungs. Now I was ready to work on the tape and rope pinning my hands together. I chewed and tugged with my teeth, ignoring the pounding of my head, stopping often to refill my lungs with oxygen.

Eventually, the tape and the knots began to loosen. I cheered myself on with every movement of the restraints, concentrating all my strength on that tiny area. For those few moments, it became my whole world. All my senses were focused on being free.

I thought of the animals caged in those walls just beyond here, unable to move around, denied the ability to roam or be loved. Was Angel born here? Had Nat rescued her from this life, picked her from dozens of others, to give her life? *Seems she was his favourite*, Walter Ryeburn had mumbled at me, head down, eyes not meeting mine. Had he known about his son's proclivities? Had he known about the puppy mill? Was he one of the partners? The one Nat had feared? If so, what was he doing a prisoner, here, with me? Who were the people downstairs? My mind refused to answer any of my questions. I couldn't think and tug and pull at the same time.

When the last of the rope and the tape snapped, I almost didn't believe it. I stared at my red swollen hands as if they were not mine. Then I shook myself and started on my feet. My toes and heels tingled and stung badly as I tore at the restraints. My fingers ached from the effort. Freedom suddenly meant pains shooting through my feet and calves. I doubled over, stretching and groaning, trying to rid myself of the prickles that tore through my veins. After a few moments, the pain began to lessen and I was able to sit up and look at my surroundings more carefully.

It seemed that we were definitely being held in an attic, probably one of the barns or sheds, as the roof was makeshift and rotting. There were no animal sounds or smells from here, however, which was confusing. It was a small area, filled with insulation and wooden two-by-fours. I knew I had to be careful to stay on the planks or risk falling through the ceiling. I sat very still, listening, hearing nothing but the distant wind and whimpering of the dogs in the compound. Then I began to crawl toward Walter Ryeburn.

He was very pale and cold. His breathing was shallow and fast. I tried to waken him by whispering in his ear, by gently shaking his shoulder. He smelled of urine and vomit. His clothes looked torn or frayed, but it was hard to tell, as he was huddled in foetal position. There was some dried blood that had come from his ear and stuck to his cheek. His hands had turned blue from the restraints. But it was definitely old Mr. Ryeburn. I knew I had to get help for him or he could die up here.

As I crawled forward over the planks, hand over hand, I realized that the space was actually a kind of loft. A few feet from where we lay, the attic gave way to the room below. I could see right into the small building. It appeared to be some kind of treatment centre. A large flat table gleamed with a stainless steel finish. A huge file drawer had been carelessly left opened and I could see the hint of instruments inside. Treatment for what, I wondered? Killing off the most diseased? Weird experiments on the most helpless? Anger propelled my bruised body into action.

Cautiously I leaned my head over the edge of the loft. No one inhabited the room, though a ceiling light blazed. I wasn't sure if anyone was around to see me, but I decided I had to take the chance and swing down onto the floor. When I hit bottom, a sharp pain went through both my legs, even though I had crouched appropriately in the jump. I lay on the floor for a moment, shivering and clenching my fists. Then I crept on hands and feet to the door, unable to trust myself upright.

Just as I pulled myself to a standing position and made ready to try the doorknob, I heard the noise of feet outside on the gravel. The dogs began to howl and cry. Someone was coming toward this building.

CHAPTER 23

Fear proved to be an even better energizer than anger. I quickly found the light switch, plunged myself into darkness, and propelled myself behind the large file drawer. I could hear a man's voice, heard the sounds of hands at the door, felt rather than saw the door swing open.

"Is anyone here?" the voice demanded, loud and angry, used to being in charge.

Relief filled my throat and eyes. For a moment I couldn't move. "Emily Taylor! Are you here? Answer if you can."

I burst from behind the files, sobbing, barely able to croak, "Yes, yes, I'm here, I'm here."

Edgar Brennan stood with a gun in his hand, pointed straight at my dark figure. I began shouting hysterically at him, not daring to take a step forward lest he mistake me for an aggressor, it's me, it's me, it's me. At once, he lowered his gun.

"Emily! Are you okay?" Then, over his shoulder, "She's here, Will!"

Suddenly my husband was there, stumbling toward me and I toward him. We wrapped each other in our arms, rocking instinctively to soothe. Tears covered Will's shirt and my face.

Edgar switched on the light and stood next to us, eyes lowered, muttering. "What the hell did you think you were doing?" was at least one of the sentences I caught.

We separated and the three of us huddled a moment, as if words could not sustain the shock.

"What the hell is this?" Edgar seemed to have a need to describe everything in hellish terms, not inappropriately, I thought.

My voice was shaky but the facts were firm. I told them about Walter Ryeburn upstairs, and as Edgar found a ladder propped against one wall, and placed it against the loft, I filled them in on the dogs that I glimpsed imprisoned here.

When Ed disappeared over the edge of the loft, I squeezed Will's hand. "How did you find me?"

"I followed you." He might have been sheepish about this, though the fact that I had been doing something very dangerous negated any regret he might've had. "I heard the door shut, went downstairs and read your message. By the time I threw on clothes jogged through the streets, I could just see you disappearing across the canal around the bridgeman's cottage. When I got to the house myself, I couldn't find you anywhere. I looked in the backyard, in the shed, and then I started banging on the doors. I had this irrational idea that Nat had risen from the dead or Walter had come back and was holding you hostage."

"I called Edgar on the cell and he raced over. Together we eventually found your walking stick and then the path. We decided to walk along, or run is more like it, to see if we could find any trace of you. Luckily, from the rain the other night, the pathway was pretty muddy and the bicycle tracks shone in the moonlight like a beacon. We saw the light on in this building, then it went out and...Emily, what the hell do you think you were doing on your own?"

Will's question was interrupted by Edgar's appearance at the edge of the loft.

"He's pretty bad. I've called 911 and for back-up from Ottawa."

It didn't seem to take much time before the entire compound was lit up with lights and the blinking of police cruisers, yet it was dawn by the time Walter Ryeburn was loaded into the ambulance. Afterward, with me leaning on Will and leading the way, we accompanied Edgar and Constables Ducek and Petapiece to investigate the other buildings. It was a far worse sight in the light of day.

The dogs were living in cages with no bedding. Their paws were covered in abscesses from standing on the unforgiving hard wire. Crusted, oozing eyes stared out at us with fear and distrust. They growled weakly, howled and cried as we passed by, sometimes baring teeth that were brown and cracked. Some of the dogs' fur was so mangled and mangy that their skin had turned into a mass of red scabs. The poor creatures hobbled painfully around their small spaces, trying to keep their balance, trying to see what these newcomers would bring to them. Dogs were crammed three or more to small cages that were elevated over mounds of feces. Matted fur covered some of their eyes as they rushed toward the front of their cages, barking at these uninvited visitors.

I couldn't help recoiling at the red and white ooze covering the dogs where open sores had erupted and insects crawled freely. I showed the police the other building, where the pregnant dogs and the females with their tiny progeny lay panting. Many of the dogs were weak, appearing to be malnourished and dehydrated. Some looked as though they were puppies themselves.

Constable Ducek spoke. "I've seen one puppy mill before this one. The female dogs start being bred at six months old. When they're too weak to breed any longer, when she's maybe five or six years old, she's disposed of."

I pictured the chrome table in the cottage. Did they put them to sleep there? Or simply dump their bodies in the garbage? Did they cut them up, squeeze their little hearts…?

We went through the building with the assortment of animal stalls. I dared not give voice to the things that probably had been done here. Judging by the silence as we passed through, they had all figured it out for themselves. The diary was no longer a fictional account. It was all too real. It was the odour, the sound and the sight of suffering, degradation and despair.

My head had begun to pound and my knees were shaking. The shock had begun to wear off and I was feeling the effects of my ordeal. Of course Will had noticed before I was willing to admit to it. His arm around my waist was testimony to his fear that I might topple over any minute. The unspoken questions about the voices I'd heard swirled around inside me. I couldn't think clearly enough to pinpoint why they'd been familiar. I was sick over the discovery of this puppy mill in our own community.

I was disgusted with myself at ever having believed that Nathaniel Ryeburn was an innocent, well-meaning person. And I was not only angry with a dead man but with two people whom I must surely have met at some point in the two years I'd been in Burchill. I shuddered to think that they might even be parents of students in my school. What would that do to our little town?

Constables Ducek and Petapiece were, I was happy to note, very concerned over my pale countenance and about my safety. They led me through a thorough but kind questioning, signing and recording of my statement. By eleven that morning, they sent me and Will home in a police car, which then stayed in our lane way, where the officer could see anyone approaching our property.

Langford Taylor brought me tea in bed, a sleeping pill, and held me until the sweet oblivion of a deep sleep overtook me.

CHAPTER 24

The medication avoided any dreaming, but when I awoke I didn't feel refreshed. I was depressed and sluggish, unable to conjure up any energy sources at all. My husband wisely said very little, providing coffee and food and newspapers (which hadn't got hold of the story yet, thank goodness).

I hadn't missed much weather-wise for sleeping most of the day. More rain drizzled down on Burchill, in keeping with my mood. By four o'clock in the afternoon, the sun had poked its way back through the clouds, bringing a silver tinge to all the raindrops and the lake.

A police car still sat in our lane way. I could almost feel the action that was taking place not very far from my little oasis. Puppies and mother dogs were being tended. Some had already been removed to veterinary hospitals and the Ontario Society for the Prevention of Cruelty to Animals.

The police combed through the property, looking for the names of the culprits of this devastation. In my imagination, I heard the questions and the whispers of the villagers. I heard the media jumping into their cars and heading back to our small town.

Angel slept, sat, or lay by my side all day, as if she felt my distress and was doing her best to comfort me. Every time I petted her and looked at her beautiful face, tears came to my eyes and I was thankful that somehow, somewhere deep inside, Nathaniel had cared enough to rescue at least this one little dog. *'She was his favourite,'* Walter Ryeburn had said, but the sinister way in which he had made that statement now led me to wonder what abuses Angel had suffered.

Certainly both she and her mother/sister had been beaten with a flashlight, judging by the reaction of both animals when that instrument was produced, even innocently. The physical abuse of the older collie had turned her into a snarling, suspicious beast, where her younger version was sweet and affectionate. I wondered if any of the more elderly dogs were still open to love and kindness, or whether they had been damaged too severely to be able to make a healthy human contact.

Just after five o'clock, May and Alain came to the door, accompanied by the police officer, a huge bowl of chili and bannock, as well as several bottles of wine. Once they were admitted, I spent a long moment in May's embrace, tears flowing from both of us.

Over dinner, Will and I told our friends everything, assured they wouldn't tell anyone else until the media had the story and the police had done their research. It helped to lay all the dirty facts out in the open, to hear and see the reaction of these two dear people, and to be enveloped in their friendship.

May shook her head, as she would do many times during the evening, and said, "I just can't reconcile the Nathaniel we knew and the one who did all this. It's as if two completely different people inhabited his body."

"I think that's exactly the way it was," I responded. "Somehow, whatever there was in his childhood, all that rejection, turned him into a Jekyll and Hyde."

"But there are so many children who suffer worse and don't turn out that way. What made him so ugly, so twisted?"

I loved listening to Alain's soft French Canadian accent, the way he tripped over the TH's, his quaint formality of structure. "It's hard to say what triggers turn a human being into a monster, isn't it?" he mused. "You hear some of these stories of real heroes, who overcome such misery and abuse, who turn into exemplary people. Then there are the others who appear to have pretty normal upbringings, who then morph into killers. There's a lot to be said about being born with a certain disposition, I think."

Langford said, "I agree. For some people, the rejection that Nat felt would have made them more determined to prove everyone wrong, to become someone they'd have to look up to. But some weakness in Nathaniel, or some weird inclination, turned him the opposite way. He used power over animals to make himself feel like a man."

I took another spoonful of the delicious chili, perfect for a cool, rainy day, and followed it with a mouthful of red wine. I was beginning to think that I would recover. "I just wish I could help to bring closure to this whole thing. I can't seem to remember much already. Everything is blurring. I think my mind is rejecting the idea that someone in this town owned and operated that puppy mill and even worse, may have murdered Nathaniel and killed his pony. It's all so bizarre."

Will and I looked at each other, both wondering how our lives could have taken this turn—again.

The evening was soothing, comfortable, even fun. That night I cuddled in Will's arms, Angel sighing contentedly at our feet. The wine helped lull me into a deeper, more fulfilling sleep, despite the fact that at times it was filled with dreams of crying puppies, parents' nights at school, and Nathaniel cleaning blood off the floor. I knew it was healthier to let my mind digest and sort out the images and shocks that had bombarded it.

Shortly after we'd finished breakfast, and Will had disappeared into his studio, Constables Ducek and Petapiece and Ed Brennan came to the door. I was beginning to think of them as members of the family, I laughingly said as I poured coffee for all of us. When I asked about Walter Ryeburn, Ed told me the prognosis was grim. He'd still not regained consciousness.

The four of us pored over what we knew so far. If the diary were to be believed, Nathaniel Ryeburn had been involved in some form of severe animal abuse. Someone from Burchill had seen Nat going into one of the clubs that catered to demented people who desired greater, more twisted 'thrills'. What that unknown person was doing there, we still had no clue. Either he was also into that perversion, or he simply had deduced where Nathaniel might be found. At any rate, with the threat of having his mother learn about his proclivities, Nathaniel began a partnership with person unknown and his wife (or so we surmised from the voices I'd overhead) to operate a puppy mill.

The land where the mill had been located was registered to a numbered company whose director's name was listed as 'Patricia Sinclair'. Whoever this woman was, the search thus far had only revealed what she was not an Ontario resident.

Nat's role appeared to be one of night watchman. From what I could remember, his diary indicated that he slept at the farm and indulged in his perversions whenever he felt like it. The pony had been killed presumably to close the school permanently so a search could be made for Nat's secret diary. This seemed to mean that the culprit had inside information that the closing of the school was temporary after Nat's murder. In addition, they (he/she) had to know that Nat had been keeping a memoir.

The diary had been stolen from our home. Someone had to have known I had it, but I insisted that I had told no one. Had someone been spying in our window? Had I been seen reading it?

Somehow Walter Ryeburn had discovered the puppy mill. Had he stolen the diary? The mill owner had caught Walter, beat him rather severely, and tied him up in the attic of the cottage. From the snatches of conversation I'd heard, they had planned to either 'finish him off later' or leave him to die. They didn't appear to feel any threat from me, as I hadn't seen them.

This line of thought prompted me to state that they couldn't have known I'd read the diary or they'd definitely want me silenced. Again, we were led back to Walter Ryeburn as the thief. But the police had discovered no diary in the bridgeman's house or at the dog compound. Where was it hidden and did it reveal the name of the culprits?

CHAPTER 25

The morning passed quickly in thought and discussion. A guard would remain stationed outside our home until the danger appeared to be over, which made me feel both relieved and anxious.

Edgar gave me a quick, uncharacteristic hug as he left with the Ottawa police officers. He also warned me that the media had begun to descend on Burchill. A press conference was scheduled for Saturday evening at the puppy mill. Our village would be spread out all over the television by tomorrow night.

Will continued to work in his studio throughout the afternoon. He had a few showings in July and August, and wanted to be prepared. I forced myself to make calls to parents, teachers, and Connie Cicero and Peter McGraw, updating them.

Despite the fact that the discovery of the puppy mill appeared to remove all fears about the school being a target, the school board didn't revisit their decision to keep it closed. Burchill was under press scrutiny and the board members were of the opinion that it was best to err on the side of caution.

They did give permission to open the school for Wednesday afternoon and evening next week, the last week of June, for parents and students to collect belongings, for our Grade Eights to say good-bye, for class lists to be distributed. We would invite our graduates back to the school in the fall for a formal graduation. I worked on an invitation to be given to the latter and on a second newsletter to update and cheer our little school community.

All communication was posted for next day delivery. It hadn't been easy to put out comforting words and cheery invitations, but it helped to look forward to the future, to convince myself that September would really bring a new year. Hopefully the summer would serve as a buffer between the horror and our quiet village life. I could scarcely fathom that exactly one week ago today I had jogged to school feeling ordinary and safe.

Ironically, on Saturday morning, a memorial service was held for Nathaniel Ryeburn at the church he'd attended every week with his mother. The entire village was there, it seemed to me. Almost reverently, they spoke of his gentleness, his dedication to his aged parents, his work at the bridge and at the school. I held my head up and smiled, nodding to parents and others, putting on the best show I could. Having had a great deal of past practice, I could disguise my feelings well, though I didn't seem to be doing a good job of it lately. I was able to use my principal face to give away nothing but the appropriate flashes of grief, anger (at the murder in our town, our school), mutual admiration (of the Nathaniel these people knew at least). I sat with Will, May and Alain, and Marj. Bill was tied up at the Mill, she told us. They were preparing for the 'onslaught' of reporters and animal rights activists.

"Well, at least it's good for something," I murmured, partly tongue in cheek, as I squeezed her hand.

"What do you mean?"

"Just..." I looked into her eyes and realized I had offended her. "I just mean that at least it's good for business. I didn't mean you were happy about it, Marj. I'm sorry. I guess I will do anything to try and find a bright side."

She squeezed my hand in return, but it was weak and shaky. "I'm sorry, too, Emily," she whispered back. "I guess I'm frazzled by all of this. Our usual clientele are people we know, mostly come back year after year. This would normally have been a fairly quiet month. That sounds all pretty self-absorbed and lame, doesn't it?"

I shook my head sympathetically. "We've all experienced some very weird feelings, Marj. I don't think any of us can ever be prepared for something like this." *I should know*, I wanted to add.

We were quiet after that, listening to the pastor extol the virtues of this man everyone thought they knew. How would they feel when (or if) the truth was revealed?

May and I gave each other several meaningful looks throughout the service. I thanked my lucky stars I had her confidence. Alain was silent the whole hour. He looked devastated. I wondered what demons Nat's murder and subsequent revelations had awakened in him.

I knew Alain's family life, as a boy, had been harsh and often cruel. It was the reason they had decided on remaining childless. Alain was terrified of his own temper, afraid he'd repeat the sins of his father literally.

Although May had had some initial doubts about never becoming a mother, she once told me frankly that she'd put all those regrets past her years ago. She was far too selfish now, she'd said. She and Alain were too close to allow anyone in. Besides, they were busy with lives they cherished. All the excuses sounded plausible.

But sometimes, I'd watch May with a hurt little one at school and I'd privately mourn both our unborn children. Then I'd remind myself that, had we babies of our own, we might not have so much to give these other little people who really needed our support and affection.

Reverend Whitmarsh's voice rolled over me like waves on the ocean. I sensed the overall feeling he meant to convey, but I found myself unable to listen to the details. I couldn't bear to see Nathaniel Ryeburn again as the town 'counsellor', the revered bridgeman, the kind and gentle caretaker. My heart couldn't take any more hurt, confusion, anger and grief at the moment.

I thought of Walter and Annie Ryeburn lying in separate hospital beds. What was going through their minds at this moment? Was Annie even aware that a service was being held and what did that mean to her? Did Walter's mind still function? I closed my eyes against the murmur of the pastor's voice and the answering mutterings of the crowd gathered in this small, hushed place.

Who had murdered him? Who had been his partner in that hellish business? Who had broken into my home and read that diary?

I sat up suddenly in the pew as though someone had poked me from behind. For no apparent reason, a fragment of memory followed the diary and me to the Inn that day for lunch. I pictured the small brown book on the floor of the restaurant. I watched May pick it up. I saw Marj, Michael Lewis, Teddy Lavalle, Diane West, Dr. Ron, Basil Fisher, Peter and Ellie Smallwood, Nick and Mary Jo Samuels, couples and singles, filling the tables, all staring at me, staring at *it*, watching as I fumbled and apologized.

I groaned. One of these people had to be part of a couple that had formed a partnership with the devil—or were devils themselves.

CHAPTER 26

Over the weekend, we watched our little Burchill being surrounded by television crews and cameras and lights. We saw with dread the surreal images of dogs and puppies being hauled out of their prison at last, some of them snarling and crying, some of them sedated, some of them meek and afraid.

Our community did not fare well with many of the reporters. The fierce opinion that 'people *must* have known. This place has been here for years' was insulting and hurtful. It was shocking to discover through television reports that the compound had existed for a very long time, but how long it had served as a puppy mill had not yet been determined.

'Investigations were continuing' was an oft-repeated phrase. They were 'following a lead' that might give them information about the pet shops who'd bought puppies from Burchill. They had not yet discovered who the salesperson or persons had been.

'Someone had information,' the reporters repeated and we were besieged with police PR voices over the radio and television asking that someone to come forward.

An anonymous tip line was established. The first tip, that an 'unnamed' man and woman had been discovered at the compound but were not thought to be part of the operation, had cost Langford and me a sleepless night. How long before I was identified? How long before our life here was over? So far, no one had found Walter Ryeburn, or me or connected the murder of the caretaker to this new event, but it didn't seem possible that it would be long before someone connected the dots.

After the service on Saturday, Will and I had spent the weekend huddled once again at home, mesmerized by the flashing lights of the television set, our window blinds uncharacteristically pulled tight. When we were not sunk into the couch with Angel at our feet or snuggling between us, we were each doing our separate best to keep depression at bay. Will spent several hours in his studio, 'just cleaning', he admitted later, because no inspiration could break through.

I spent that time in front of my computer, staring at report cards, trying to see the children behind the words, trying to remind myself that the world, indeed, was still spinning and carrying on the way it was for most people. We both were mourning the loss of our safety, our security, our haven. Our unspoken lament—for us, will things ever go back to what they were?—kept us preoccupied and even silent. We couldn't put the feelings into words just yet. The idea was too scary, too bruised, to touch.

Monday and Tuesday dragged by in the minutiae of details. I finalized report cards, made and answered phone calls about Wednesday's arrangements, ensured that staff were kept up-to-date. I typed, read, wrote, organized. Wednesday's social busyness came as a welcome relief.

Langford had an important meeting with a studio in Merrickville, a small town to the west of us, which was the site of his July showing. He was reluctant to leave, as he would probably not arrive home until after midnight. I assured him that I would be immersed in the school until late this evening and would have Alain escort us home.

May and I had a ton of report cards to print, not to mention setting up for the reception of parents and students from 5 p.m. to 9 p.m. at night. We had purposely given parents a four-hour window in which to get home from work, pick up kids, or take care of other tasks and still have time to visit the school. I had pulled some funds from my budget, unspent on the many events that should have taken place in June, and hired Marj and Bill to provide munchies, juices and coffee. I wanted everyone to feel welcome, comforted, and normal in the school again, even if I myself wondered if I ever would.

The day passed in glorious, almost 'mindless' trivia. The only startling reality that stopped us in our tracks was the cleaning crew who'd been sent by the Board to give everything a scrubbing, a crew that no longer included Nathaniel Ryeburn, not to mention the brand new carpet in front of our offices.

May and I gave each other a long look, but didn't speak of it. We rolled up our sleeves and went back to work, as if delving into physical, menial work would distract us until all of this horror went away.

By the time 5 p.m. arrived, May and I had the school ready, decked out with pictures and trophies and flowers. Report cards were stacked in the classrooms. Teachers had their spiels rehearsed, along with an appointment schedule for those who wanted interviews over the next few days.

Marj and Bill had provided a huge assortment of sandwiches, cakes, cookies, fruit and vegetables with dip, all grandly delivered by Teddy. Marj and Bill had even offered to pick everything up after nine to avoid any cleanup for the staff. The tables were covered in blue and gold cloths to represent the school colors.

As soon as people began arriving, the gym was teaming with people eating and talking and laughing. There was a video playing in the gym of our myriad of sports events and other happy occasions that had been taped throughout the year. The Grade Eight students had made a display of their final elementary days with personal pictures and testimonials to be friends forever.

They were, I was surprised and pleased to note, excited to be holding their graduation celebration in the fall. It was an opportunity to return, and besides, that's the way graduating secondary school kids and university students did it! We had decided on October 3, and invitations were given out by our fresh-faced young ladies and gentlemen, who were nonetheless scarcely able to hide their delight at graduating early and the prospect of a longer summer vacation. Parents, on the other hand, grumbled and some complained loudly. Once again, I was glad to have had the school board take the heat on this one.

The presence of Edgar Brennan, Constables Petapiece, Ducek, and two other uniformed police officers reminded everyone that, despite our attempt to normalize the situation, it was definitely not business as usual. Their quiet, authoritative watch at each entrance served to temper some of the parents' criticism of the closing of the school. I was kept busy, however, all evening, meeting with those who questioned the Board's decision, others who felt their children had not received their full education this school year, and some who just wanted to express sympathy.

Burchill's small town community was very different from the city, though. I had found the students here to be mostly innocent and naive in comparison to my schools in Vancouver's east side. The parents were, for the most part, supportive and enthusiastic about their school and the staff.

By the end of the evening, I was filled with a sense of happiness and buoyed by the spirit of the children and their families. I was tired, yet energetic at the same time, filled with hope for the future. Maybe everything would go back to normal, after all.

Marj and Bill arrived as promised at 9 p.m. They, too, looked tired and ruffled, having spent another round of days with reporters and curiosity-seekers banging on the door of the Inn.

Strangers to our village! Intruders, not even tourists. Speaking badly of our town. It was funny to me how easily I had stepped into the role of a villager, viewing all people from 'away' as potentially damaging to our peace and quiet. Ironic, considering the fact that I now knew that someone within this village was the source of all the horror over the last few days.

When Alain arrived to pick us up, there were a few stragglers left. Some parents, including Ruth McEntyer, organized the Grade Eight display, still putting pictures away carefully to save for graduation. A few people helped to clean up the leftover food. One group continued to talk as though they didn't see one another on a daily basis.

May and I stood in the doorway to the gym, suddenly sighing at the same moment.

I laughed and put my arm around her shoulders. "May, you go home with Alain. You've done lots more work than I have, and I'm the one who gets paid the big bucks. I'll ask Marj and Bill to take me home."

May, reluctantly cajoled by Alain into accepting my offer, gave me a hug and was gone. I hadn't wanted May to know, but I had decided I was fine to go on home by myself, even if going into an empty place was a bit daunting. Then I remembered the little four-legged creature who would be there to greet me and I smiled. It was already hard to even remember life without Angel, and she had been with us for only a little over a week.

I straightened my shoulders and used that one last burst of energy to talk to the remaining parents, help with the food cleanup (not much left over though, I was glad to see), and wave good-bye to the last staff and students.

"Mrs. Taylor, this was such a great idea," Ruth rambled on, careful not to use my first name in front of the children, as though they didn't know it already. "The community feels so much better. Thank-you for doing this."

I smiled and mumbled that it had been a combined effort, but Ruth kept right on yammering. I moved closer to Bill and Marj, thanking them for their contribution, trying nicely to dislodge Mrs. McEntyer from my side.

"Thank-you both so much. This food was delicious—a huge hit. It went a long way to making people feel comfortable. And I *know* you gave us way more than we paid you for, so don't try to tell me differently."

"You're welcome, Emily. It's our community and we like to give back where we can," Bill said formally. His face was puffed and red. His eyes were encircled with dark smudges.

He'd not had much sleep with all their invaders, I thought.

Ruth McEntyer came up beside him and gave Marj a hug. "You are amazing. Doing this for the school while handling all the extra work at the Inn. We are ever so grateful!"

I could see Marj trying to politely disentangle herself. Her eyes, too, were puffy and dark with sleeplessness. She looked at me over Ruth's shoulder and I gave her a sympathetic smile.

Eventually, by about 9:45, the remainder of the people had left, even Ruth McEntyer. Marj and Bill were loading tablecloths and trays into their van, while I turned off lights and locked doors.

I was coming from my office, having secured everything there. The Percivals were back in the gym, collecting the final remnants of the evening.

I stopped just outside the doors to the gym.

One voice was female, high pitched with anxiety, the other male, nervous, shaky, gruff. Gone were the British accents. The flat, understated tones of purely Canadian-born took their place.

I recognized them at once. The voices from the cottage at the puppy mill.

They were whispering to one another, but in the cavernous emptiness of the room, their words were clear.

"She knows. I'm sure she knows. Did you see the way she looked at me?" Almost squeaky, high-pitched, shaking.

"She doesn't *know*. She's not looking at you funny. You're falling apart. Get a hold of yourself." He, stiff and formal, anger seething underneath. "She would have told someone by now if she knew. We wouldn't be standing here in the school if she suspected, you ass. She's a goddamn goody two-shoes, you know that. And a bloody busy body on top it all." The sound of a tray banging against the table. "*You* are going to be responsible for anyone finding out, idiot. You've been acting stupid. If you don't watch out, you will be the one I'll have to get rid of."

I stood frozen, just on the other side of the door, when they emerged. Frightened, shocked, nauseous, I could not force myself to move.

Bill and Marjory Percival stood and stared at me, the trays incongruously stacked in their arms. Then suddenly Bill moved, the trays crashed loudly to the tile floor, and his big hand clasped my arm with bruising force.

"*Now* she knows, you bloody idiot," he flung back to his wife, who stood shaking, tears flowing down her face, still clutching the detritus of a celebration.

And still I could not move, could not take a breath, could only stare incredulously at the hand squeezing my arm. When I did breathe, I felt dizzy and ill from the sudden intake of oxygen. My mouth began to work again.

"Bill, Marjory...how could you? Those puppies, Nathaniel, the pony..." I was stuttering, blithering, not making any sense.

"Shut the fuck up." Bill Percival's face was flushed with anger and frustration. He was no longer the jovial innkeeper. His eyes flashed with cruelty. He was clearly enraged at this turn of events.

"If you had kept your mouth shut," he hissed, turning to his wife, who still had not moved or made another sound, "we wouldn't have had to deal with this. And if *you* had minded your own goddamn business..." He spat at me, too furious to speak further.

With a shove of his leg, he swept my feet out from under me. I fell hard on the tiles, first my hipbone and then my chin crashing onto the floor. Pain seared up my spine and through my head, forcing my eyes shut and a screech of anguish to come bubbling from my lips. The toe of his boot swung back and struck against my ribs. My breath came swooshing out. Mercifully my consciousness shut down before the second kick reached my pain centre.

When I opened my eyes again, I knew that I had never felt such agony before. My chest hurt with the pounding of my heart and the shallow breaths that I was able to gulp.

Bill was slapping me hard, making my head sear with pain. A ringing began inside that dulled my hearing.

"Get up, bitch, or you are dead here on the floor of your school like that bastard of a caretaker."

He yanked on my arms until I was on my hands and knees, trying to get the breath and strength to stand up. I knew somehow that this was what he wanted and that I must obey, but my body screamed at me in protest. My knees gave out once, but suddenly I was upright, trying to keep my eyes open in the fluorescent glare.

As if she had heard me, Marjory turned off the hall lights, plunging us into the eeriness of the night-time lighting system. Their faces were ugly and smeared with hate, the dim red emergency lights striping their eyes as they moved quickly around either side of me.

"We'll take her out the back into the van. The lights aren't bright there and there are no houses backing onto the yard. We'll get away, Marj, stop blithering."

They goose-stepped me down the empty hallway, pinning me close to them with their hips and arms. I shuddered in horror, distaste and discomfort, unable to propel myself without them, toward a new terror that my mind refused to even ponder.

Bill Percival kept talking the whole way, reassuring his wife, telling her they were going to get away with it, they'd head to the airport straight away, he wouldn't kill me.

"Marj, it's okay, I don't want more blood on my hands. I didn't even mean to kill Nathaniel, you know that. He just wouldn't listen. And the old man, he deserved it, you know that too, Marj. But if you don't want me to kill this bitch, I won't, I promise. Just stop the crying, please. I can't take it anymore, Marj. You're acting as if I wanted all of this. We'll just put her where they won't find her until we're gone." But I didn't believe him, and I could sense that neither did she.

Bill shoved the back doors open, where the blackness of the inside of their van yawned in front of us. Marj twisted sideways through the portal, still clasping my arms. I could hear her whimpering and sniffling, could see the tears glistening on her face in the moonlight. My mouth could only handle the tortured breathing. I couldn't ask her why.

CHAPTER 27

"Stop *now*, Bill." The voice blasted out from the quiet schoolyard, close enough that all three of us jumped. "Don't make it worse than it is."

And Edgar Brennan stepped around the van, his gun in his hands, pointed at our absurd six-legged team. From the other side, I saw Constable Petapiece, her gun steady and aimed calmly in our direction.

Amazingly, Bill Percival titled his head back and laughed, his voice echoing absurdly in the still heat of the summer evening. "Edgar, Edgar," he chided, still laughing, "how the hell could it be any worse?"

He flung my arms away as if I had been clasping him. Marj covered her face with her hands and began to sob loudly.

Slowly, as if I had been a puppet on strings, I sank to the gravel and lay crumpled there, as Edgar placed Bill and Marj against the sides of the van, their hands high, their legs spread apart, his gun at their backs. At some point, Constable Petapiece encircled me with tender arms, slowly lifting me, and before I was able to think, I found myself sitting in the back seat of an OPP cruiser.

It seemed no time passed when suddenly there were cars and lights and an ambulance in my little school's yard. Parents and students had flocked back, attracted by the noise and disturbance, and were standing shocked and silent behind a police barrier.

He had spoken several times before I was able to actually decipher Edgar's words.

"We were still in the yard, waiting for Bill and Marj and you to leave, talking about everything, just trying to mull the whole case over."

As if I'd asked him how he'd rescued me, I thought. Had I?

"Finally, when you seemed to be taking too long, I started to enter from the back doors. That's when I heard and saw you. Bill was confessing his brains out, though he didn't know it at the time. We waited to make sure they didn't appear to have a weapon on you, then out we stepped."

I think I was intoning thanks, but I'm not sure. Edgar was still holding onto my hand when I was placed on a stretcher and lifted into the ambulance. There was only one other time I had been taken to a hospital this way, and I remembered with deep fear and sorrow that Will hadn't been with me then, either.

"You mean Langford?" I could hear the puzzlement in Edgar's voice and suddenly I wondered what I had spoken aloud. "I've called his cell phone, Emily. He's on his way. He'll be there at the hospital soon. I have to stay here, get the questions answered, do the paper work. You're in good hands, Em. I'll see you both very soon."

Later, I remembered only bits and pieces of the trip to the hospital, images and touches and pain. Faces filled with concern and kindness seemed ethereal. Hands and needles and darkness and light swam past, until finally I slept, long, hard, dreamless.

Langford Taylor, his pepper hair askew on his forehead, his lips touching my hand, his eyes filled with love, was my first image when I awoke. My body felt slack, bruised, but warm and supported. I sighed, drawing a long comforting breath, so filled with gratitude at the life to which I had been returned.

Will smiled and kissed me gently, then sat on the bed, his hand still clutching mine. Never, never let go.

"It was Bill and Marj. Langford, can you believe it? Is this real?" Several tears escaped, rolling salty onto my lips.

Langford shook his head, keeping his eyes on mine. "I know, Emily, I can't believe it either. I haven't got the whole story yet, but Edgar promised he'd come over soon. You've been asleep for about fourteen hours. The doctors said that's what you needed. Luckily, there's no concussion, but a couple of your ribs are broken." His voice stumbled, caught. "That's why it probably hurts to breathe."

I smiled slowly at him. "Actually, I must be pretty well drugged up. I don't feel too much at all." I gently explored the wrappings around my body with my other hand. "How long do I have to stay here?"

"Just a couple of days, honey, just to make sure you're healed enough to come home. Then I'll take care of you, Em." A couple of silent tears rolled down my husband's face. "I am so sorry all of this has happened to you. I shouldn't have gone away."

"Langford, don't. None of it is your fault. Some of it was mine for being so nosy. Curiosity killed the cat, remember." I put my finger on his lips, swiped at the tears. "It's going to be okay, that's what matters."

I moved myself slowly and carefully over to the other side of the bed and Langford gingerly lay down beside me, his head on my shoulder, our arms wrapped around each other.

We stayed that way until a nurse cleared her throat from the foot of the bed and then I endured a round of pokes, prods, and temperature gauging. She brought us both hot soup and coffee, which we gratefully sipped as we talked and smiled at each other.

The dishes had just been taken away when Edgar Brennan knocked and came into the room, his arms full of flowers.

"You might as well be prepared, Emily. Stephanie said their shop has been inundated with requests for bouquets for you. I think we'll have to get you a bigger room."

"My hero!" I beamed, taking his hands in mine. "Edgar, I can't begin to tell you how grateful I am."

Edgar Brennan actually blushed. "Just doin' my job, ma'am," he chuckled, pulling up an empty chair and sitting. "But I must say, it was just dumb luck that Frances and I had stayed there. It wasn't like we had a premonition or anything. I was just nervous about everything that had happened, and to tell you the truth, I thought it more likely we might be invaded by reporters wandering into the school while it was still open. Frances was the one who suggested we stay until everyone had cleared out. We had parked at the other side of the school, so I guess Bill presumed everyone was gone. His lips were sure loose enough! I actually overheard everything, including his confessing to killing Nathaniel. Do you feel like hearing the whole sordid story, Emily? Langford?"

We both nodded our heads vigorously. I settled back to listen, but not before registering the fact that Constable Petapiece had become 'Frances' and that her name had been mentioned several times. Edgar had been a widower for a number of years now. I wondered if he might be interested in another woman at last. Didn't he say that they had been 'parked' outside the school?

"Percival has been working the puppy mill for a lot of years, even before he married Marjory and bought the Inn," Edgar told us, obviously distancing himself by never again referring to the innkeeper as 'Bill'. "It seems they did this kind of business in Great Britain. Though they're not actually English. They're from parts unknown at the moment, but England must've been where they learned those accents. Percival is a first class creep. We're checking into his record from London and I have no doubt there will be some pretty interesting stuff. It gets worse, though."

"Even before the puppy mill, apparently Percival and his cronies had had some kind of club going. It makes me shudder to think of it. Our little town, surrounded by sickos who wanted to abuse animals. A few years ago, apparently Ryeburn convinced Percival that to continue with the club was too dangerous. There were a lot of mental deficients who had found out about them and visited there. Who could trust *them* not to tell? Besides, both Ryeburn and Percival had decided to quit their disgusting habits. He said it as if they were quitting smoking or something for heaven's sake!"

Edgar had to stop here and get his breath. All three of us sat open-mouthed at the depravity of the human soul.

"So instead they opted for the more lucrative business of selling dogs to unsuspecting pet shop owners. Marj claims she hadn't a clue about the bestiality club. She claims she came into the picture with the puppy mill. But apparently she was quite happy to be the salesperson. Whenever she went into the cities supposedly to buy supplies for the Inn, she cheerfully sold dogs to various pet shops. Of course some of the shop owners were a little reluctant to admit that they'd bought from her. They probably suspected all along, but we've found a couple who are truly horrified and who are willing to testify that Marj Percival was their sales agent."

"At some point, Percival and Ryeburn had a falling-out. It looks like Ryeburn had been wanting to quit the puppy mill operation too and Percival wouldn't let him out of it. There was some kind of huge argument, during which Ryeburn threatened Percival and told him he had a diary that would prove everything, so don't think about retaliation. In fact, Ryeburn confessed, his son knew everything and that was why he wanted to shut down the mill."

"His son?" Will and I spoke at once, looking at each other and at Edgar in astonishment.

"Nathaniel didn't have a son, did he?" I asked stupidly.

For a moment Edgar was speechless, then he nodded knowingly. "Sorry, sorry, Emily, of course. I didn't clarify. It was Walter Ryeburn who was Bill Percival's partner."

CHAPTER 28

'I am the bridgeman, as my father was before me, and as his father had been before him, down the ages of my family history like a brand.'

Nathaniel Walter, not Nathaniel Junior, the author of those words, the son whose tortured life had brought him to abuse and be abused. Walter, in love with the beautiful Annie, unable ever to believe that she could love him. Somehow she'd had the patience, the love, the insight, to break through his barriers and convince him that he was worthy of love. Yet after she married him, gave birth to his child, he could not bear to let her out of his sight lest she change her mind, and all of his insecurities and mental weakness had resurfaced. He'd turned their home into a virtual prison.

How sad and ironic that their son had turned out to be just like his father in appearance and, or so it must have seemed in the teenage years when he too ran away, in temperament. Yet it was Nathaniel who gave real love to animals, and who had respected and loved his father until he discovered the diary, the sordid past, and the cruel present. He begged his father to end it or he would have to go to the police.

Annie, confined to a wheelchair and at last completely and utterly in her husband's hands, would have to be left behind. Walter, in his distress and anger, had sealed his son's death when he screamed the facts in Bill Percival's face.

Bill had accosted Nathaniel, followed him to the school, trying desperately to talk him out of turning his father in. How could he put his own father in jail? How could he deny his father this extra money? They weren't really doing anything wrong—who knows all the ways Bill tried to dissuade Nat? Who knows why he pulled out the gun and shot him? Who knows why Bill Percival cared nothing for the lives of the people around him, and the animals in his charge?

Will and Edgar and I sat for a long time in the hospital room, listening to the faint sounds of tending to illness in the background. I remembered our conversation with May and Alain about evil and the puzzling fact that one person turned to monstrous acts while another, from the same roots, remained good and kind. Walter and Nathaniel, the bridgemen, both born into torn and troubled relationships, both saddled with the mantle of confessor, the responsibility of a small town's traditions. One had retained his humanity and his soul. The other had traded it all in, surrendered to impulses that debased and degraded himself and the people he touched. Yet how cleverly both had worn the mask of innocence, each portraying a different face, each hiding concealed strengths and weaknesses, undisclosed evil or goodness, honesty or deception.

We all have a mask to wear, I thought, some more hidden than others. My husband and I were not so different, after all, except perhaps that we were painfully, daily, aware of our secret selves.

"Walter was the one who killed the pony and broke into your house, or so Bill claims. And it does make sense, I guess. He wanted the school evacuated so he could get the diary. Even in his distress about his son, he was protecting himself."

"Maybe there was incriminating evidence against Bill Percival in that diary, too," I suggested, scarcely believing I was offering up a kind of defence for Walter Ryeburn.

"You could be right, Emily," Edgar agreed. "It does appear that Walter was obsessed with getting Percival. He was convinced that Bill was the murderer, though his partner kept denying it. Apparently Walter was following Bill around, threatening to expose them both, claiming he didn't care what happened to him any longer so he had nothing to lose. Bill said he promised Ryeburn that he would shut down the puppy mill in Nat's honour, but pleaded to get rid of the rest of the current shipment. He coaxed Walter out to the mill one more time, where they really got into it, and Bill beat the older man to a pulp. Where Walter put the diary, we still don't know and may never." Edgar sighed. "Walter died in his sleep last night."

Both Langford and I made some inconsequential noise, something like 'huh', not able to feel pity or sorrow at his passing, still remembering his cruel and indifferent face as he shoved Angel into our doorway, or as he paraded his captive wife in front of us.

I was mourning Nathaniel all over again. I wondered what thoughts had run through his head as he faced his killer. I marvelled at the strength that had propelled him to defy his father. No wonder he had been clutching the picture of his parents and his pets. Even in death, he had wanted to protect the safety and dignity of the animals. I was certain he'd been trying to leave a message. If only I hadn't assumed that the diary was Nat's! How could I have thought that the shy, country, innocent, boy-man that Nathaniel was could have written such a treatise? It seemed ludicrous now.

"They've still got Annie Ryeburn here in the hospital. I don't know what's going to happen to her once she's well enough to be released. She did say she has a younger sister in Manitoba, so maybe she'll go there. I do believe her when she says she knew nothing about it. I don't think Walter or Nathaniel told her a thing."

"From what I remember of the diary, I would say silence was their way of dealing with all their problems. I doubt that they really talked to each other or told each other how they were feeling." I squeezed Will's hand. "They never knew true intimacy in their lives. How sad."

"Yah, true I suppose, but it still doesn't excuse their actions." Edgar stood up. "I'd better let you go, Emily, Langford. I've actually got other things to do. Now that everything is out in the open, the reporters are having a field day. Especially since most of them are still staying at the Inn!" He laughed loudly, enough to catch the disapproving eye of a passing intern.

"I just can't help but think of how ironic that whole deal is," he continued. "It seems Teddy Lavalle isn't just the chef, he's a partner. Bill Percival actually offered him his percentage of the ownership out of the blue a few days ago—surprise, surprise—and Ted was just arranging for the financing. However, Teddy doesn't seem to be involved at all in anything sordid. So he's running the Inn on his own."

"The police have ransacked Bill and Marjory's apartment upstairs at the Inn, but nothing so far. I think they burned all the evidence in anticipation of flying out of the country. I guess they figured as long as no one had put them in the picture, they could pretend to sell out and return to England or wherever. Good thing Bill confessed without knowing it and decided to brag about everything in front of other witnesses. Without that diary, we might not have been able to get all the facts. Now we don't need it. We have enough from his own lips to put him away for the rest of his sorry life."

"What will happen with Marj?" Will asked.

"I don't know exactly. She's been charged as an accomplice to murder and for cruelty to animals and so on, but who knows what a defence lawyer will do? Maybe she'll claim wife abuse."

Edgar left us, still shaking his head and muttering. It was good to see the strain of the last week leaving his shoulders, even though there was still a lot to face.

Langford and I knew that we might have reporters on our heels for a while, but the village would protect us, and in a few days some other murder or equally horrible event would take the spotlights away from Burchill. Maybe we'd even be able to get back to normal.

The next evening, after I'd been up and around, carefully, all day, I wandered out into the silent hospital corridors, my robe tucked around me, my slippers making swishing sounds as I cautiously made my way through the hallway.

Her room was on the floor below, so I took the elevator, feeling the drop of my rib cage a little too heavily as it clunked downward. No one said anything to me. The hospital was quiet and sleepy, exhausted from the daily ministry to illness and pain or by the excitement of new birth or the titillation of emergencies.

Annie Ryeburn was in a ward. All four beds contained willowy, celestial bodies, their faces turned away from the door, as if looking beyond the world to the place where they'd soon be taken. I saw her long flowing grey hair swept up on her pillow, and went to sit on the chair beside her. She looked at me calmly, her eyes wide awake and clear, as if she'd been waiting for me.

"You're the one he liked," she said, her voice soft and gentle in the night.

I nodded. "I guess so. I'm certainly one of the people who liked him."

"But you were the one who made him feel good about himself. He always would tell me that you asked his opinion and told him he did a great job." She turned her head so that she could see me better, her hands fluttering up and down the buttons of her nightgown. "Do you love his Angel, Mrs. Taylor?"

I smiled. "Please call me Emily. We love his Angel very much. And she seems to love us. I can't believe how quickly she adjusted to us and how affectionate she is. Now I can't imagine life without her. She's become a member of our family." I paused. "I'm so sorry, Mrs. Ryeburn. You've lost so much, and here I am rattling on about a dog."

"It's Annie, and that's all right, dear. I know you mean well. Besides, your having Angel and loving her makes me feel so very much better. Nat would've really liked that. He never thought of her as just a dog, and

I know you don't either. Then there are some people who don't think animals have feelings at all." She averted her eyes from me, staring at the ceiling as though picturing her son, as though he were looking down at her.

"Did—was Angel beaten?" I asked, my voice breaking.

"I don't think so, my dear, but I'm sure she was born at that terrible puppy mill. There's no telling what she witnessed. Nat rescued her when she was very young. He kept filling up our yard with abused and injured animals. Little did I know where he'd gotten most of them from."

She sighed deeply, her chest obviously heavy with guilt and regret.

"You know the funny thing, Emily? I loved Walter. I know he was odd to everyone else and not handsome by a long shot. But I loved him. I married him. I had his son. I told him over and over again that I would never leave him. But he never believed me. He made me his prisoner instead. Eventually, God forgive me, I wished him dead every single day. He wasted and ruined the life we could have had. I guess he never thought he was worthy of it."

I am the last true bridgeman. I deserve no more than this ignoble end.

"I wouldn't let him ruin my boy, though. Nathaniel was good and sweet and kind. A little slow, I guess, not a thinker, you know. But decent." Tears swept down her cheeks, lying in the crevices of age, pooling around the creases in her neck. "And maybe he would've found someone to appreciate him. I always wanted to be a grandmother."

I joined her in tears then, reaching out to hold her hand in mine. We cried gently, grieving the loss of what was and what could have been. When the tears stopped, we sat for a long time in the semidarkness, listening to all the breath in the room. Life continuing.

"Emily," she spoke suddenly, no tears in her voice. "Do they have any proof about Walter?"

I was startled by the change in her tone, officious now, her hand removed from mine. "Edgar said since they couldn't find Walter's diary and they couldn't find any written records of the puppy mill or the..."

"The beast club," she said, each word clipped with disgust. "And I name it after the humans involved, not the poor animals."

I could only nod my assent. "It's only Bill Percival's word that Walter was involved."

"You have to get rid of the diary. You have to protect Nathaniel. Even though he's gone, I can't bear for people to know about his father, and to think of that every time they think of my son. That sick old Bill Pervertival can go ahead and say anything he likes."

I had to smile in spite of myself at Annie's turn of phrase.

"But I don't want Walter to confirm the dirty rumours in his own hand," she finished.

"But the diary is gone, Annie," I repeated. "No one can find it. Because Bill confessed, Edgar says they can get a murder conviction without it, so I doubt Walter's part will even…"

I stopped as she sat up, seeming lithe and energetic for the moment, and reached over to the hook beside her bed for the giant purse hanging there.

Rummaging around inside for a moment, she finally held up a little brown leather book. "How did you…?" I asked, startled.

She shut her eyes, the tears squeezing through her tortured lids. "Walter killed that poor pony. He broke into your home. How could he?" I held her trembling hand for a moment, and then I understood.

"You didn't fall down the steps that night trying to get your medication, did you, Annie? It was the diary you were looking for."

"He was an idiot for recording all of this in the first place. This filth. These excuses. I loved him. Why couldn't he accept that? Why couldn't he leave the demons behind and enjoy our life?" She shook her head, sniffing, her fists curled in anger. "I always thought there was something lacking in me that I could never give him security." I started to protest, but she held up her hand. "No, I know, his baggage was too heavy. And I was too pretty and too popular. He spent the first few years of our courtship and marriage in a daze, following me around like an anxious mother, staring at me as if I were an apparition."

"I hauled him from party to party, from neighbour to neighbour, celebrating. He could never see that I was celebrating our love, this amazing man who was so intelligent and funny and caring and gentle underneath that ugly make-up. I wanted everyone to see what I saw, not just the surface. But it only made people understand less and talk more. It made him more insecure than ever."

"After we had Nathaniel, he seemed even more terrified, for now he had two people to lose. And because his little boy so resembled him, was also given the burden of ugliness, Walter wanted us all to crawl inside a cocoon and never emerge. I kept trying to tell him that looks didn't matter. It was the inside that counted. If only he had believed me. If only he had known that his inside, that part of him buried way, way underneath all the crap and the things he'd done in the past, was wonderful and beautiful."

"If only he'd had the fortitude to tell Bill Percival to get lost. If only he'd known that even if I had found all this out years ago, I would have forgiven him. I would have still loved him. The one thing I could not forgive was the way he imprisoned me and our son with his fears."

She fingered the worn leather for a moment, her head down. "Poor Nathaniel found this when he was just seventeen years old. He and his father had a huge row and Nathaniel disappeared. He was gone almost five years. According to Walter, the club had been disbanded and we were both ill, so Nathaniel agreed to return. Walter neglected to mention the puppy mill that was going strong by then. You cannot imagine my joy and my sorrow at seeing my son. I had had so many dreams about where he was, about the new life he was living. I wished they'd all been true."

"Nathaniel eventually found out about the puppy mill and told his father he'd better get rid of it, or he'd go to the police this time. When Walter told me all this the night before he disappeared, I hadn't a shred of forgiveness left in me. I like to think that he was trying in his stupid way to plot revenge for our son's murder, though. I think the pony was killed as much as a signal to Percival as it was to get into the school and search."

"You could be right, Annie. You should have seen Bill's face when I told him about the pony. At the time, I thought it was odd. But how did Walter know I had the diary?"

"After he'd searched the school thoroughly, he was convinced someone from the school had it. He'd seen your kindness when you came to visit us and when he took Angel to you. He suspected you might be the recipient of Nathaniel's confidence. I don't know how he knew exactly, though. Maybe he was spying on you. Who knows what he was capable of? The last thing I said to him was that he was a pathetic excuse for a human being."

A shuddering sob rose up inside her, but she stilled it with a breath of strengthening air.

"I refuse to feel guilty about that, my dear. My husband put me and my son through too much for me to end the rest of my days feeling sorry. If only I had known about the beast club, the puppy mill. If only I had left him years ago, when his paranoia became intolerable, maybe my poor little boy…"

She was silent for a moment, breathing shallowly, her eyes closed again. When she opened them, her voice was stronger.

"There is only one thing I can give my Nathaniel now. I want him to have a good reputation. If Walter gets dragged into it by that monster, he deserves it, but the story will never really be confirmed, unless they have this diary. I lugged myself down those stairs, hauled my ass up onto a chair to reach it. I never thought I had that kind of strength in my upper body!" She gave a small, ironic chuckle. "It's amazing what you can do when you need to. And I counted on the fact that our Burchill-born Edgar wouldn't search this old lady's purse."

"Without the diary, you can cast doubt on any of the stories, can't you, Emily? You can tell the people of Burchill who like to talk about things that the bridgeman was an innocent, drawn into the horrors by the likes of the fancy pants Percivals and that you bet most of what old Bill has to say is lies. Then pretty soon it will be spread everywhere and it will be believed. After all, the Percivals weren't born to Burchill like the bridgemen were."

She held the diary out to me. "If this is gone, they'll never prove it. There'll always be doubt and everyone will just remember the wonderful parts of Nathaniel and maybe even Walter."

"You could tell them yourself."

"No, it would sound defensive. Besides, I have to leave Burchill. I'll return in my casket some day. In the meantime, my sister Sara wants me to be with her. She's been a widow for a while now. We can both enjoy her grandchildren, I hope, and take care of each other. I can't burn this filth, either. I'm stuck in this wheelchair for life. No, it has to be left up to you."

"But I'm not Burchill-born. I'm a true stranger here."

Her eyes fixed on mine. "Oh, but you have the soul of a Burchill native. And you had Nathaniel's high regard and devotion. You'll do right by him. Besides, you know the people who will spread the word." She winked. "Like that Ruth McEntyer, the waitress, you know?"

I chuckled softly, holding the diary tightly. "I'll do right by Nathaniel, Annie. Thanks for trusting me. And for giving me Angel." I leaned over and kissed her on the forehead, startling her, ignoring her instinctive reaction to pull back. "I think Sara's grandchildren will be very fortunate to have a second grandma like you."

CHAPTER 29

It was the middle of summer, one of those for which central Ontario is famous—hot, clear, with the kiss of lake and river in the breeze. It was unlike the clamminess of Toronto or the rain-soaked days of Vancouver. The air was California fresh, as if we could walk to the ocean from here. My ribs had almost completely healed and I felt my old energy returning as I walked over the bridge toward the cemetery.

The trials of William and Marjory Percival were still months ahead, stuck in preparatory motions. The two of them were vying to see who could tell the best story. Marjory was indeed laying all the blame on Bill, asserting that he beat her and intimidated her into doing his dirty work.

The puppy mill had been cleared away, leaving nature to crawl back and sit upon the empty land, bringing the life of smaller, freer creatures. Sadly, many of the animals had been unable to survive their ordeal and were reluctantly put to sleep.

The Ontario Society for the Prevention of Cruelty to Animals had moved in to assist those dogs and puppies who were still open to trust and who were healthy enough to be adopted. People from Burchill and all over the province opened their hearts and their homes to these poor little souls. We all learned a great deal about puppy mills and how to avoid inadvertently supporting them.

Later that year, a certain 'Den' in Toronto was uncovered and quietly razed. Most people in Burchill still don't know about that aspect of the incident and I truly think it's better that way. Such evil does exist in the world, but I'm not sure we can totally eradicate it, and I have to believe that only a minority of people sinks to such levels. So I wasn't about to reveal the entire sordid story to anyone.

The village Inn was undergoing some renovations, just enough to leave behind the taint of Percival tastes.

Frances Petapiece was often seen in town, sometimes hand in hand with Edgar Brennan, watching the ships go through the locks.

The bridgeman had been replaced with a computer and a series of electric switches, which one of the villagers had been hired to oversee and repair. No one seemed inclined to stop and talk with him. He was all business, a computer geek they said. The bridgeman's house had been sold to the town as a heritage site for one dollar and was going to be turned into a museum.

Annie Ryeburn moved away quietly, with no one to wave farewell. She took all her belongings and her memories, hopefully the good ones.

Somehow the rumour got started that Bill Percival had lied about Walter Ryeburn all along and that the old man thought he was working to help the animals instead of harm them. Even further, it was said that Walter Ryeburn had no idea of what actually went on at the mill until that fateful day when he went to see it, and got beaten to death for his efforts. By the time the villagers were finished with the story—which, if truth were told, they never did tire of telling—Walter and Nathaniel Ryeburn were practically heroes.

It didn't really bother me that Walter had gotten away with so much, at least in the eyes of the villagers. He had paid for his sins with his life, in so many different ways, even as he lived. As long as Nathaniel was known as kind and brave and innocent, I made my own private judgment that the scales of justice were even.

Edgar had been right when he said that they had enough on Bill and Marjory to put them away for life. They didn't need the scribblings of an old diary. Even the leathery bits had melted in the large fire I'd built in our back yard.

Before burning it, I'd peaked inside at the very last page, at the words written by this tortured man not so very long ago. The growing distrust of his wife's love, his terror at losing her and his little boy if they ever discovered his past proclivities, leapt from the pages.

In his twisted way, he had thought the puppy mill would be a better use of the land. He'd actually believed they would treat the dogs with kindness, or at least with self-serving attention and care. But Bill's greed led them to overproduce, resulting in neglect, torture and abuse, something Bill Percival (Pervertival, somehow I liked to recall) seemed to enjoy.

Walter had stopped recording in the diary long before attempting to remove himself from the puppy mill. He had, however, made it very clear who the lead in all this despicable activity was—one William Percival. After reading it, and following the Ryeburn legend as it grew throughout the village, I was secretly pleased that the rumours about 'heroism' were a little closer to the truth than I'd imagined they could be.

The cemetery is very old. It was originally divided into two distinct sections, one that served as a burial ground for the reservation, and one for the rest of the folk. Now, we are all together in death, even if there are still barriers in life. I walk to the end of the eighth row, where a small monument stands just to the left of a tree. Nathaniel has his own space here, his own testament to his life. N. Walter Ryeburn, Senior, lies three rows over, waiting for his wife, who will someday finally prove in death that she will always be with him.

I sit down on the warm, dry grass and pick a couple of tiny weeds, placing my new, fresh flowers in the little vase that popped out from the marble.

'*Nathaniel W. Ryeburn, Junior, the last true Bridgeman*' reads his epitaph. Ruth McEntyer has informed me that, in the last few days since this headstone was completed, many people have visited Nathaniel's grave. They stand, or sit as I am, talking to their bridgeman. I don't tell Ruth that I think they should leave him alone. In actual fact, I never knew if Nat liked his role or not. Perhaps he did like listening. Perhaps he is happy that people still wish to confide in him, give him their trust. And Nathaniel was certainly deserving of that honour.

I stand and look toward the ice blue sky, the creamy clouds, the birds drifting above. Perhaps Nat has even made peace with his tormented father by now.

A crow boldly circles my head. He settles on the tree next to Nathaniel's grave, straightening his wings and gazing peremptorily around the cemetery.

You know, Mrs. Emily, birds are actually very smart. Especially crows.

The crow winks at me, his head cocked to one side. He opens his beak and lets out a small, gravelly greeting.

After that crow's wing healed, he hung around people like he was one of us. I had to capture him again and take him way out to the reserve so he'd get used to the woods again. He looked at me with such hurt eyes when I told him to fly away, just turned his head sideways and listened to me talkin'. He knew what I said. He just didn't want to believe that I didn't want him around. But he was gettin' too close to the kids in the park and all the parents was complaining. I figured sooner or later someone'd shoot him. I hope he's happy out in them woods.

I stand up and look back at the crow, smiling. If anyone is looking and listening, they might think, appropriately perhaps, that the school principal has lost her mind.

"I hope there are animals and birds where you are, Nathaniel, our last true bridgeman," I say to the crow, who continues to look at me sideways, eyes blinking as if he is listening and reacting to my words. "And I hope you're happy too."

With that, the bird lifts his huge black wings and sails upward, circling the cemetery for a few minutes, and then heads into the sun.

Here's a sneak peek at book 2 in the Emily Taylor Mystery series...

VICTIM

*We, like the birds, fly in a certain direction,
and in spring, the jackrabbit starts his way.
Through the hare's eyes, I see.*

PROLOGUE

Frieda waited until the police had finished searching. She did not even make the journey up the road until all the sightseers and relatives had drifted back to their homes. By the time she began walking toward the house, the woods had gone back to their natural quiet.

The sun made diamond patches on the crisp snow as she trudged up the hill. Overhead, several birds circled, silently searching for mice indiscreet enough to take a run through the leafless trees. Frieda's breath came in puffs of white clouds and the cold tingled her nose into a reddish blush. Crunching across the brittle ground, Frieda's eyes and ears told her countless stories about life in the forest.

Just to the side of the road, a small rabbit had been seized by an owl. Frieda spotted the frantic tracks racing to the trees, the sweep of the bird's wings as it grazed the ground and then flew off with its prey. A little further on, Barry Mills' son had destroyed a sparrow. She could see the boy's footprints and then a smattering of feathers and blood, which had once been a bird. Frieda smiled at this. Bobby Mills was learning to be a real hunter.

The thrill of the hunt shivered through her body. She could picture the huge deer she had caught last week, flattened against the snow, eyes bulging and fearful. Waiting, felled by the pain, the victim was at Frieda's mercy. It was left up to her to end the misery, to decide between life and death. At that moment, she was the one in control. She was the god, the arbiter of fate. For Frieda, the power of those moments was the reason she loved to trap and hunt.

The native woman prided herself on her keen powers of observation. She had spent most of her life in the woods, first trailing after her father, the man whose quiet aloofness had taught her to be silent and watchful. Her mother, frail and self-pitying, always lay pale and sighing in her bed when they arrived home, scrutinizing her daughter as though Frieda were an object of great perplexity. Frieda would spend hours in the woods alone, too, or in the shed out back, abiding by the stern lessons that her father had taught her about skinning and drying animal carcasses.

Later, when she was almost a grown woman and her parents had died, Frieda followed in Oona's footsteps. At the thought of Oona and the traps, her heart swelled with pride. Oona had shared her knowledge with anyone she thought worthy of it, and Frieda had proven her best pupil. Together, Oona and Frieda had travelled and camped in these woods several thousand times. They knew it the way most people know their living rooms. The two women had similar builds—strong and stocky, muscular and round from walking and hiking through hills and forest. They could scale walls and ford streams, build campfires from scratch, and create wooden structures that withstood most storms.

Frieda stopped at the bend in the road and sniffed the air. She might have been a bear whose den was being threatened, for only when she did not hear the saw whining in the distance or smell the dust of a fallen tree did she relax her stance. Her round, serious face was creased with sun lines and now, worry and curiosity. Her small brown eyes were inquisitive, almond-shaped, overshadowed by thick eyebrows. Her gaze was disconcerting to most. She had the ability to freeze conversation with her stare. As far as anyone knew, due to the woman's irascible and detached nature, Oona had been Frieda's only friend.

The layer of ice that had fallen over the snow yesterday must have thwarted their efforts to build again today. Frieda smiled maliciously. Along with other Ojibwa natives and Burchill residents, Frieda hated the encroachment of the new subdivision on their communities. As most of the villagers did, Frieda dreaded the increased population as an intrusion on their quiet way of life. But she had other reasons for her reactions. Although the threat of competition in the trapping business was very real, Frieda was also secretly energized by the idea of a more modern life. She had her own secret agenda and the guilt made her uneasy and filled with anger. She knew, however, that the subdivision was not destined to last. Not if she could help it.

The winter this year had not lent its sympathy to those opposed to the construction. Instead, it had been unusually warm, with very little snow, allowing the contractor to continue building. Over the last three days, a blanket of snow had coated everything, and then a sheet of ice had fallen on top. It was probably the first time in history that the Burchill Village residents, native and non-native alike, had welcomed the snow and cheered an ice storm.

By the time she came within sight of the camp, Frieda had warmed to the hunt. Her breath was steady, the blood pumped excitedly through her veins. She went first to the little house. The door was open as always. Frieda stepped into the quiet warmth and waited until her eyes adjusted to the dim light.

Everything was as Oona had left it. The rusty kettle sat abandoned on the black pot stove. Her cup, crusted with tea stains, perched nearby, a withered bag curled, forgotten inside. Oona's gun, shining and ready, gleamed from the corner.

Frieda went in slowly, touching everything, drinking in the silence of the cabin. She thought she could see the outline of Oona's body on the thin mattress of the single bed. The cupboards were simple and few, constructed of raw wood that had never been finished, although each cup and plate and foodstuff had been organized neatly inside. There were utensils for only three, a small aluminum table with two uneven, unmatched chairs and one rocking chair with the stuffing held inside by duct tape. Even as she took in every object in the small room, Frieda found herself thinking of her own new home, and of how foolish Oona was to live this simply when she could be living in comfort as Frieda was now doing.

She pictured Oona sitting here, smoking the wooden pipe that had been in her family for centuries, avidly reading whatever book she'd been given or borrowed, her face barely illuminated in the light of the kerosene lanterns. Slightly taller than Frieda, broader at the shoulders and hips, her face wide and open, her eyes impossibly large and disingenuous, only Oona had been able to defrost—at least temporarily—the frigid gaze that Frieda turned on the world.

The real friction had stemmed from her guilt, Frieda knew. She had betrayed Oona's friendship, taken advantage of her innocence and trust. Her eyes flitted involuntarily to the old cupboard, its marred wooden surface spotted with age, sagging against the crooked floor. She remembered what she had done, and conflicting emotions darted through her mind. Misery, pride, joy, fear and guilt all struggled to reopen her closed heart. She blinked and turned away from the little room.

Pulling on her mittens Frieda plodded back out into the cold, following the tracks carefully. The sheer layer of ice covering the snow had moulded the prints clearly into the ground, as though they had been painted there. Despite the dozens of footsteps made by the police and others, Frieda was able to find the ones she wanted. Straight and sure, the tracks proceeded emptily in a straight line away from Oona's camp on the edge of the reserve, toward the forest. Just before the big rock, the prints stopped abruptly. It was here that Henry, out looking for his sister, had found Oona's old brown coat. Covered with snow and ice, it had been abandoned and flung in a heap next to the rock. A small distance to one side, Henry had discovered her mittens.

Frieda paused here, studying the efforts of the police and the others from the village. It took several minutes of careful observation before Frieda could sort out the correct prints and take up the trail again. They headed directly toward the forest, further apart now, obviously running. Frieda followed them quickly, feeling the pace, imagining some fear that would have made Oona run.

When they reached a huge pine tree standing alone at the forest edge, the tracks suddenly veered to the right. Frieda stopped and stared, amazed at what she saw.

The prints raced around the tree, not once, but exactly twenty times, in ever-widening, almost precise, circles.

CHAPTER 1

May received the call at 10:30 on a Monday morning. It was a testimony to our friendship that she ignored my obvious, selfish reaction when I found out she had to leave. Somehow, Monday mornings at Burchill Public School were always hectic, unpredictable, and well, as the song goes, rainy days and Mondays always got me, the principal, down.

This particular Monday was packed with events. A raging, purple-faced parent absolutely refused to even listen to anything I had to say. Luckily, we didn't have many of those in town, and as the villagers would say, they tended not to be Burchill born. A child languished in the health room with a suspected broken arm, but her parent seemed to be taking the long way here. Three students, who'd been caught throwing snowballs at a fiercely barking dog on a neighbour's property, were currently writing out their sins at the table in the office. Two classes were being temporarily watched over by other staff while May had begun scrambling to find supply teachers. Our caretaker was busily deciding between mopping up a leaking toilet and checking the temperature gauge in the gym, which was even too cold for running. Not only that, it was one of those frigid, damp days on which central Ontarians expected their babies to be kept indoors, which had already prompted several frantic calls to the office. Not being Burchill born myself, I am sometimes seen to be far less knowledgeable about things like weather than I ought to be.

So when May Reneaux, my only office assistant, got the call telling her that Oona had disappeared, my first reaction was to dismiss the news as another of her aunt's prolonged hunting trips. However, I knew in my heart of hearts that Edgar would not have called May at work if he thought Oona had simply gone off on her own.

Edgar Brennan was in charge of the Ontario Provincial Police (OPP) detachment in our area. His official title was Chief Superintendent, but we always simply referred to him as the town's police chief. The detachment served our village of Burchill, the First Nation community adjacent to the village, and the provincial park on the other side, as well as the highways that led into the area. Edgar was Burchill born and raised and had worked all his adult life here, so he knew his people very well. If he thought Oona was on a hunting trip, he would never have sounded the alarm by calling May away from the school.

It was not easy to hide my displeasure from May. She had become a very close friend in my four years in Burchill, especially over the last two. She knew me extremely well. However, she was too upset to notice my mood, and luckily when I realized the depth of her distress, my selfishness dissipated, and I made her exit fast and easy.

I spent the entire morning soothing ruffled feathers, checking the weather station, escorting the supply teachers to their classrooms while giving them a quick course on the school's policies, assisting the injured child until her parent strolled in, eliciting apology letters to the neighbour from the snow-throwing boys, calling the school board about the broken gymnasium heaters, and answering the telephone. Two of our most reliable Grade Eight students came down to the office to help over the noon hour, but even with their eager assistance, I was unable to take a breather until later in the afternoon.

I sat at my desk, contemplating this school principal job. Never had I felt so dissatisfied, even though, on the surface everything was going well. I began to drift in my reverie, wondering about the source of my unhappiness and bitterness lately, and actually started guiltily when Dominic, one of the office helpers, told me Mrs. Reneaux was on the line. I realized that I hadn't thought about May all day. When I heard her shuddering intake of breath after my hello and inquiry about how everything was, I knew the news couldn't be good.

Speak, speak to me, all the air, land, water,
speak to me while the earth
locks us together.

CHAPTER 2

Frieda shook herself and began to follow the tracks, her heart racing uncontrollably. She pushed the fear to one side, taking deep breaths of the cold morning air. She began to concentrate on the skills needed to follow the tracks. Definitely, she found that the prints wound around the tree twenty times, very close together, obviously at great speed. Yet they were precisely made so that they created wider and wider circles. Frieda was puzzled. On the last trek around the tree, the footprints raced off to the left and disappeared into the forest.

For a moment, the native woman stood absolutely still, listening, thinking. Her round face, framed by long, straight hair that refused to turn grey, looked mesmerized. Suddenly, she bent down and took an object from inside her coat. Digging with her knife—the exercise difficult in the semi-frozen ground—she eventually made a large hole alongside the tree. Frieda placed the object inside and carefully put the dirt and bits of debris back where they had been. Straightening, she was pleased with her work. No one would know that anything had been placed here. The searchers were finished with this spot and would never think to come back. Somehow, Frieda knew that she should not take the treasure into the woods with her. Her decision had been made. She was going to follow Oona, and if she found her former friend, she did not want the burden of that object to hinder their encounter.

Mixed with the tracks of the police and villagers, Frieda almost lost Oona's prints several times. Slowly, keenly, she followed them into the trees right up to the edge of the large pond. Here they stopped abruptly, as if Oona had stepped off into the murky water and disappeared through the thin layer of ice, which had closed like scum after her. The police and villagers had spent much time here, tramping off in every direction, wading into the shore of Bahswaway Pond.

Frieda stood and sniffed the air, staring around at every tree and bush, feeling the atmosphere. It was deathly still, as if every animal and bird were in hiding. No breeze stirred the lifeless limbs. Though she stood silent, Frieda's mind was racing.

There had been talk by the villagers that Walking Bear had frightened Oona. They surmised that he had found her trapping and had chased her into the icy water.

Frieda did not believe in Walking Bear, but an ancient fear gripped her anyway as she surveyed the scene. Ojibwa children of Frieda's generation were still taught the lessons of the past. She had been raised with stories of spirits that existed in every animal and in each leaf of every plant. She knew the legends of the various clans. She had been ingrained with the notion that sorcerers could arrange with the spirits of the earth to bring punishment upon humans who disobeyed the laws of nature. As an adult, Frieda had rejected many of the native ways and beliefs, but now in the hush of a winter forest, the little girl in her still shuddered.

Quietly, she inched along the edge of the pond, studying every twig of every bush along the way. Her feet slid over the ice without a sound. Her lithe body brushed against nothing as she manoeuvred through the trees. A short distance along, Frieda found the first evidence. It was a small bit of fur, drenched with dried blood, caught on a twig of one of the bushes. The fear grew larger and pulsed through Frieda's head. It was the fur of a bear that she held in her hand.

CHAPTER 3

"It looks as if she might have drowned." May's voice shook, as she fought off the tears that threatened to silence her. "Henry found her coat and mittens strewn all over. Her footsteps headed straight for Bahswaway Pond and disappeared. But, Em, get this. The footprints wound around a tree twenty times in these weird circles before she ran off into the water. You should hear the stories that are going around. Our people are still very superstitious during a crisis, it seems. I haven't heard some of these legends since I was a little girl."

I sat back in my chair, stunned, thoughts racing. "My God. But isn't Bahswaway just a pond? Wouldn't it be frozen up over the last couple of days?"

May gave a rueful chuckle. "I keep forgetting you're not Burchill born, my friend. That's why it's called Bahswaway—the Echo. The story goes that it was once a huge well that the natives had dug and then abandoned after several children disappeared into it. A pond formed around the well, but it's still very deep where the hole was. It doesn't actually freeze all the way down apparently, even in severe winters. The legend could actually be true, or maybe it's not. But at any rate, the pond *is* very deep in the middle—" The enormity of what she was reciting suddenly caught in her throat.

I leaned forward. "It's so strange, May. Those footprints, everything. What does Edgar say?"

"He doesn't know what to make of it. Everybody's puzzled as hell. Oona's house looks just like it always does, pretty neat and tidy. It's almost like she's going to come back at any moment. It doesn't look like she'd planned any kind of trip, especially a hunt. Her rifle is still there. And anyway, she always lets me know if she's going to be gone for very long."

Although May's mother had been a wonderful, caring person, she had not wanted her daughter to grow up in the *old ways*. It had been her Mother's sister Oona who'd taught May to hunt, fish, camp and cook in the traditional native ways. May had always felt very close to her aunt, especially when her mother suddenly died at fifty-eight—an age that was feeling more uncomfortably young to us every day. Oona was now seventy-five years old, although she looked and behaved more like a woman in her fifties. She was still active and spent a great deal of her time in the forest around Burchill. May and I had enjoyed more than one camping trip with her, enthralled by her tales of nature and native lore. Oona was a fascinating person. She was quiet but powerful, able to captivate an audience for long periods of time with her Oral Traditions.

May looked a lot like Oona with her long hooked nose, oval face, straight black hair, light brown skin, large black eyes, all in a short, compact frame. At first glance you might think that Oona and May were overweight, until you noticed the hidden power of their hands and arms and the muscles in their shoulders. Her people had been built for carrying water, wood and dead animals, May would laugh. Too bad she'd been born when she had. Her self-deprecating humour is just one of the many things I love about May Reneaux.

"But the footprints go right into the pond, and with her coat and mittens being abandoned, it just doesn't look good, Em. Edgar is organizing a search party right now. We've got lots of volunteers among the reserve and the town alike, which is really gratifying."

"Everyone loves and respects Oona. She's a towering presence in this community. If something has happened to her..." I trailed off, aware that I was not doing much to cheer up my poor friend. "And if something hasn't, she's going to be really pissed that there's a whole bunch of people coming to find her!"

May laughed. "Won't she be, though? I can just see her face!" She sighed. "Thanks, Emily. You can always make me feel better. I just hope we find her and that she's still alive."

"May, don't come in tomorrow. I can ask Gillian to fill in for you. You're going to want to join the search."

"Are you sure? I hate to leave you in the lurch like this."

"You're not. Really. Gillian will be fine," I assured her, hoping that it was true.

I could hear the relief in her voice as she thanked me. We hung up after I'd promised to see her tonight. As soon as we'd done so, I got on the phone again and called Gillian Hubbard, one of our amazing, generous parents who sometimes helped out in the office. She was quick to say yes, having heard about Oona and wanting to support May.

The rest of the afternoon flew by with far fewer problems. By the end of the day I felt almost normal and had decided not to quit my job after all. I waited until the building was mostly deserted, and then headed home on foot. Most days I did walk to and from the school. In the warm weather I actually jogged. But today I'd had no choice.

My husband, Langford Taylor, was a painter of some note in the region. He had left very early yesterday morning for a showing in a nearby town. In a place like Burchill it would be unforgivable to have two vehicles, and since I didn't expect him until late tonight I was stuck with my own feet as transportation. I planned to return home, change, feed the dog and head over to May's house, but it didn't quite turn out that way…

Read book 2 in the Emily Taylor Mystery series...

Ancient evil comes in many forms...

School principal Emily Taylor is caught up in the inexplicable disappearances of two well-known woman and the violence linked to a disputed land claim.

When the legendary Walking Bear appears, she must also deal with the resurrection of an ancient legend and the terrified and unnerved villagers of the sleepy town of Burchill.

Once again, Emily is drawn into the unknown and must battle her own secret demons and fears. Only then, can she can unravel these mysteries—before there is more bloodshed.

Available from Amazon and other retailers.

Message from the Author

Dear Reader:

This is not an easy book, because of the terrible way that animals are treated. Unfortunately, the scenarios are steeped in truth. I hope you will plough through those sections, to get through to the message: that human beings might all be capable of evil, but very few really act upon those urges, thank goodness.

There is, in the end, hope for all people and for the world for which we should be acting as shepherds. My admiration to all those who care for abused animals.

According to the Society for the Prevention of Cruelty to Animals, there are approximately 300 puppy mills in the province of Ontario alone.

Here are some tips on what you can do to help shut them down:

ADOPTION from the SPCA is the only absolutely certain way to avoid inadvertently supporting a puppy mill. REPORT any case of animal abuse, neglect or suspicious living conditions to your local SPCA.

LOBBY by joining in the letter campaigns that are initiated from time to time through the SPCA websites. DONATE to the registered charitable SPCA organization in your area (you can get sympathy cards when a beloved pet dies, for instance).

—Cathy

About the Author

Catherine Astolfo retired in 2002 after a very successful 34 years in education. Catherine received the Elementary Dufferin-Peel OECTA Award for Outstanding Service in 1998. She was also awarded Dufferin-Peel Catholic Elementary Principal of the Year in 2002 by the Catholic Principals Council of Ontario.

In addition to her career as an educator, Catherine is a qualified trainer for the Myers-Briggs Personality Inventory and spent many years speaking and leading workshops, both in business and in education. Thus she is comfortable presenting to adults and children alike, described by her colleagues as a "dynamic, fascinating speaker."

Catherine has always aspired to be a published writer. She can recall writing fantasy stories for her classmates in Grade Three. Her short stories and poems have been published in a number of small Canadian presses.

She is the author of The Emily Taylor Mystery novel series: The Bridgeman, Victim, Legacy, and Seventh Fire. In 2005, she won a Brampton Arts Award for The Bridgeman. Her short stories won the Bloody Words Short Story Award (second and first) in 2009 and 2010.

Visit Catherine at www.catherineastolfo.com

IMAJIN BOOKS

Quality fiction beyond your wildest dreams

For your next ebook or paperback purchase, please visit:

www.imajinbooks.com

www.twitter.com/imajinbooks

CPSIA information can be obtained at www.ICGtesting.com
Printed in the USA
LVOW111711110512

281392LV00025B/242/P

9 781926 997629